Also by Kit de Waal:

My Name is Leon
The Trick to Time
Six Foot Six

Becoming
DINAH

Kit de Waal

ORION CHILDREN'S BOOKS

First published in Great Britain in 2019 by Hodder and Stoughton

1 3 5 7 9 10 8 6 4 2

A CIP catalogue record for this book is available from the British Library.

ISBN: 978 1 51010 570 6

Typeset by Hewer Text UK Ltd, Edinburgh
Printed and bound in Great Britain by Clays Ltd, Elcograf S.p.A.

The paper and board used in this book are from well-
managed forests and other responsible sources.

MIX
Paper from
responsible sources
FSC® C104740

Orion Children's Books
An imprint of
Hachette Children's Group
Part of Hodder and Stoughton
Carmelite House
50 Victoria Embankment
London EC4Y 0DZ

An Hachette UK Company
www.hachette.co.uk
www.hachettechildrens.co.uk

To Bethany and Luke as always
For my niece Leah Doyle

Prologue

Cut your hair off? Not as easy as you think. You need the right stuff for a start.

Electric shaver? No. Proper scissors? No. If you haven't got them, you'd better think hard. Think fast.

First thing, get rid of the weight, get it from long to short. And if your hair lies the whole length of your back, as thick and heavy as a blanket, this could take forever. So make a start.

Grab a great big hank of hair, wind it around your hand and pull it upwards, away from your scalp. Go carefully with the redhandled scissors, the ones that you took out of the kitchen drawer that your mum uses for cutting coupons out of newspapers or cutting the string off a parcel. They're not sharp and the blades are bent but it's all you've got.

So get in close as you can. If you'd thought about it you might have bought a hair cutting kit from somewhere but you didn't think and anyway the nearest shop is seven miles away and this is

1

happening right here, right now, and it's too late for wishing what you might have done . . .

You cut. And you cut. You have to do this over and over again, cut and cut and cut, hair on the left, hair on the right. Chop into the top sections, pulling and cutting and trying not to leave any long bits as you go. Ignore the tremble of your fingers and the bump of your heart asking over and over if this is the right thing to do. Because you know it is. You know it is.

The back of the head is the hardest because you can't see. Balance a mirror behind you, hang it off the hook on the bathroom door. Try not to block out your own reflection or get in your own way as you snip and cut and scratch. It's hard to make your hands do the right thing when you can only see them in reverse and it takes forever and the muscles in your arms ache and the muscles in your shoulders ache and it's the biggest thing you've done so far in your whole life. Well, it was until yesterday. But you don't want to think about yesterday so you carry on.

Then when it's as short as you can get it, you stare at the new you in the mirror and you see yourself for the first time. You look like someone you don't recognise. And it's not good. But you look different and that was the point, wasn't it? All that's left where your beautiful hair used to be is clumps and wisps and wavy tufts sticking up at strange angles, and painful scratches where the dull blade of the scissors caught your skin. And even though you're tired there's still more to do.

So you fill the sink, bend over and dip your head in the water. Add a squeeze of shampoo. Make a lather on the tufts, all white

2

and soft as a cloud, and you look like an advert on the telly for someone having a really good time in the shower, except you're not having a really good time. Tough. It's too late to turn back now. You make the suds thick and creamy and you're just flying blind now because you don't really know if it will work but you've got no choice.

You get your mum's razor, the one she's been using under her arms and on her legs for months, the one with little rusty bits on the corners, the one that's been sitting on the side of the bath forever, the one you have to hope is still sharp.

You start by making long tracks along the great curve of your head and the razor keeps snagging and getting clogged up with your tufty hair. The soap stings and the blood turns the suds to pink like no advert you've ever seen.

And you really know now, you're more certain than ever that you should have had a better plan.

You rinse the razor under the tap to make it clean again and you keep going even though it hurts with all the tangles and pulls and you feel like you're on the verge of tears but you choke them down. It wouldn't take much more to make you cry. Not today.

It seems to take forever. Your arms hurt even more than before. As the suds and the lather disappear you see that your scalp isn't as brown as your face. It's not even brown at all, it's the same colour as your mum's face in winter, white and pale. Your stomach lurches. You're going to look ridiculous with non-matching skin with cuts and scratches all over the place and your eyes red from not sleeping

3

all night, or like someone who's had cancer, like someone who's dying not someone on the brink of a new life. But you stick with it, keep making tracks with the razor until the tracks take over and suddenly there are no more tracks to be made.

You rinse your head under the tap and feel the tickle of the water like cold fingers dancing on your new skin. Then you stand up and dry your face. Then you look. Look again. Look again and keep looking because it's worked. There you are. You're not boring old Dinah any more. You're someone completely new. Or you will be.

But there's no time to stand admiring your new self in the mirror. You have to clean the silky, black, wet tufts out of the plughole, pick the long tresses up off the bathroom floor, and make sure you don't look too hard because you'll wonder at the colour of your hair, like the bark of a tree, and the shine of your hair, like the sleek coat of a cat, and you'll remember the weight of your hair and the feel of it, soft and heavy against your skin, warm on your back. And you might remember all the times people said they loved it and how they wanted to touch it and how it made you beautiful and how it made you feel.

And you think about putting your hair in the bin, but you realise you can't and you don't know why so you bundle the tresses into a small, soft pillow and you take it downstairs with you and put it in a carrier bag. And you put the carrier bag in your rucksack and you put your coat on and say goodbye to the only life you've ever known.

Now it really is time to go.

1. Dinah

The nearest way for Dinah to get from New Bedford to the main road is down Tanners Lane, through the gate, over three fields, skirt the industrial estate where they make tyres, where the black smoke stings her eyes and settles like soot on the trees, under the bridge and across the island. That's the way to go. There'll be loads of vans and lorries going to Newcastle, to Sunderland, to Durham, and then south, someone's bound to stop.

But the rain has been lashing the cottage all night, spring comes slowly to the valley and great black shadows sit like ghouls on the landscape. So after crossing the fields, she'll have to make sure she scrapes the mud off her shoes before she gets into anyone's car. Start as you mean to go on, Dinah. Quiet and polite.

If she'd kept quiet, kept her feelings to herself, she wouldn't be in this position. If she'd been polite, she wouldn't be running away.

She stuffs her things into a bag. Everything is squeezed into something else: her clothes in a ugly holdall, her money into her jeans, her head shoved into a woollen hat that feels too big and baggy now. And her heart, too big for her chest, pressed up against her ribs, beating wild and hard. But Dinah has been awake all night waiting for the right time and this is it. She has to go but it's such a big step. What if it all goes wrong?

Not a sound inside the cottage. Not a sound beyond. Just the endless calling, one bird to another, the wind tearing new leaves from the trees, and somewhere far off a farm dog barks, whoops of delight at being released into the open, let loose, dashing across the land, miles to cover. If Dinah could, she would bark as loud and long as any animal. Louder.

Last thing of all, she goes into the kitchen. Twice now she's nearly fainted from not eating. It seems unimportant these days with so much going on inside. One jam sandwich, one cheese, a carton of milk, a packet of biscuits. There's no space in the rucksack so she shoves it all in a carrier bag and then stands at the front door. Get on with it, Dinah. Turn the handle, Dinah. Come on, come on. Time to go. For ever.

And to make sure she means it, to make sure there is no way back she takes her phone out of her pocket and throws it on the stone floor. It cracks and splinters. A shard of black plastic flies off and hits the door.

And then *crack!*

A bang on the other side of the wooden door makes her jump.

'Open up!'

And again, the crack of wood on wood. It's Ahab.

'Open up!'

Her heart's pounding again but she doesn't want to look scared. She makes sure her hat is covering the whole of her head and quickly kicks the broken phone under the table, out of sight.

She takes a deep breath and opens the door just as he raises a broom to bang again. He almost falls on to her as he pushes past. His long hair is matted, his trousers wet and his one leg shakes. He could be a hundred years old by the look of him. Hard to believe he's less than half of that.

His top half is all muscle. Dinah's seen him in the summer with his shirt off, tattoos up his arms and on his neck, faded cryptic messages and a rose that used to be red, a name too, 'Caroline'.

Dinah wonders if she'll get a tattoo once she's far away. She's seen beautiful white ink ones, as fine and delicate as lace, that would look good against her brown skin.

Ahab tries to lean against the banister in the hall but slips, falls off his homemade crutch and on to the stairs.

'Christ! Your mother, where is she?' The empty leg of his

jeans is soaking and black with mud. He wears one boot, the laces trailing along the carpet like garden worms. He's staring at her. 'Where's Anne?'

Dinah reluctantly puts her bags down. 'Sacred Women.'

'What?'

'The retreat. She's doing a workshop at the Sacred Women Retreat in—'

'Shit, shit, shit, shit, shit, shit, shit.' He kneads the stump of his knee, as he mutters one word after another like he's reading a shopping list.

He motions for the broom but as soon as he starts to stand, his leg shakes again, as if it's about to buckle under the weight of his body. He folds himself back on to the step and bangs the wood hard on the floor. 'Where the bloody hell is she? Why didn't she tell me? "Might be going away," that's what she said. "I might." *I might.* Not definitely. She should have bloody well told me. I need her.'

Dinah's not sure if he's angry with her or angry with her mother or just angry with the world as usual.

He holds his dirty hand out and Dinah has to take it. It makes her wince.

'Hold still,' he says. He flips the broom upside down and slides the matted bristles under his arm. He puts his other arm around her shoulder. He smells of the earth, of the pitted track where he must have fallen, of oil and grease and the enormous, dark farmhouse no one ever visits.

8

'Home,' he says as he hops to the front doorstep. 'Not fast neither,' and Dinah barely has time to throw her bags on the floor before he's shuffling and nudging and shouldering her up the track.

'Why haven't you gone with her?' he asks between his panting breaths. He steadies himself on the broom, hops on his one good leg, sways into her, hops again, and all the while Dinah bears the weight of a six-foot man on her shoulder and the slippery feel of the mud he's smeared on the back of her neck. This isn't what she wants to be doing. She should be on her way by now.

'Did you fall over?' she asks.

'You try hopping half a mile downhill,' he says. 'See how you get on.'

Then silence all the way up to his house. Silence, apart from his grunting and swearing, apart from the squelch of three boots in the black, gritty sludge, apart from the everlasting rain, bouncing off the tin roof of the barn making everything twice as slippery and twice as slow.

They get to the front door. It's wide open.

'Help me in,' he says.

Dinah has to grab him round the waist to get him up the three stone steps and into the long hallway. It feels strange to hold a grown man like he's a baby. He nods towards the kitchen and she manoeuvres him past a wooden bench as narrow as a church pew that's covered in bits of metal and car parts, along the grey carpet that used to be red, that used to have green and blue thistles and a golden diamond pattern down the middle. They shuffle through another door and finally into some warmth. A kettle steams on a big black range, chairs scatter around a square wooden table and instead of a tablecloth, layers of newspaper and more bits of metal, an enormous cog and a rusty dial. It might be warm but it's not welcoming.

He drops into a chair. 'Pass me a cloth,' he says.

Dinah picks a tea towel off the kitchen table and hands it to him.

'Wet it,' he says.

His voice rumbles deep in his chest like an old engine. He doesn't ask, just commands, and no matter how she tries, it's hard to answer back. It's hard to say no when you've always said yes.

She turns on the tap, and notices then on the deep windowsill, a bird's wing, soft velvet black with flashes of deepest blue, beautiful and out of place. She wonders what happened to the bird, how it died or who killed it. One minute it was flying free and the next? She imagines the bird falling to earth, crashing into the ground and lying still. If she had time she would say a prayer for it and she hasn't prayed for a very, very long time.

'Peace,' she whispers but that word just reminds her of the mess she's in.

Why does everything feel so wrong? Dinah's whole world is upside down, dead things and angry men and cuts all over her head that are beginning to sting.

She hands him the damp cloth and as he wipes his face, his eyes appear, his nose, his lips. He becomes human again. Just.

If she hadn't messed about making sandwiches she wouldn't have been in when Ahab knocked on the door. She would be halfway across the field by now, she would have got away.

'Will you be all right now?' she asks, walking towards the door.

He looks at her and makes a half-laugh. 'Do I look all right?' He slaps his leg, the one that ends at the knee, and waves the empty muddy cloth where his calf should be. 'Does this look all right to you? Does it?'

It's the sort of question that doesn't want an answer and anyway Ahab is the sort of man you don't answer back. One day, when she's far away, Dinah's going to stand up for herself and tell people like him what she really thinks. Not long now.

'Where is the . . . I mean, shall I get it for you?' she says.

'My leg? Where is my bloody leg? Is that what you're trying to say? Well I'll tell you where it was until yesterday.' Grabbing the table and then the work surface and then the back of a chair, he hops and stumbles to the window and points to one of the outbuildings that litter the yard.

11

'In there. It was in the workshop in the back of a white split screen.'

She follows his gaze but can see nothing. 'A split screen?'

'A van!' he says, turning to her. 'A 1967 T1 Split Screen Volkswagen Campervan in Whale White. My leg is in that bloody van!'

'OK,' says Dinah. She takes one step towards the door and then he's shouting again.

'Where are you going?'

'To get it for you.'

'It's not there now, you bloody idiot! They came and took it, didn't they? Disappeared, drove it off. Stolen. I've been working on that bloody van for six solid months, nearly finished it was. My sodding knee was killing me, still is. So I just took my leg off for half an hour. Came home. Fell asleep. Someone came and took it and I know who it bloody well was. With my leg lying under the back seat. Do you think I would have fallen all the way down the bloody track to your house if it was still over there?'

His words slap her one by one. His swearing and shouting. He's been like this for years, shouting and demanding. Nearly every memory she has of him is the same, firing his snarling, sarcastic words like arrows aimed at everyone in his way. He used to be the boss, the big man, in charge of everything, owner of everything. Well, that was then. Things have changed for Dinah. As soon as she made her plan, something clicked and shifted and this time, and for the rest of her life, Dinah can just walk away. She's got bigger problems than him. She turns and walks off.

'OK. Bye, Ahab.'

He holds his hand out towards her. 'Wait! Wait! Don't go!'

She keeps walking.

'You can drive,' he shouts. 'I've seen you! Wait!'

Dinah is off down the hallway. She thinks about going back for the bird's wing, to rescue it from him. If she had wings she would be far away by now, two black wings on her back taking her up high away, from everything she's done wrong and from angry men and angry girls and the shame and embarrassment of her mistake.

'Wait! Please!' His voice has desperation in it. She stops but doesn't turn.

'Two hundred pounds!' he shouts. 'I'll give you two hundred pounds.'

Dinah stays still, her new naked scalp prickling against the rough wool of the hat.

'Three hundred pounds,' he says. 'All you've got to do is get me south, drive me to Dorset.'

She goes to speak.

'I know, I know. It's a long way. I've got another van. You can drive, can't you? I know who took it. I know where they live. But we've got to go now. They can't have gone that far. That van can't go over sixty. We might even catch them up. Three hundred pounds. Three fifty.'

In the front pocket of her jeans, Dinah has two hundred and seventy-four pounds and some coins. She has no idea how much money she's going to need. She'll need to eat, she'll need to find somewhere to live. It might take her weeks to get a job.

'Four hundred,' she says and they stand looking at one another, the rain running down the window, the wind whipping branches against the glass.

'You used to be shy,' he says.

'I need some clothes,' shouts Ahab. 'Go on. Quick. Trousers and two shirts. Couple of jumpers too. Might be May but it's chilly at night. Need the right clothes for a night on the road. First door on the right.'

The stairs are wide and deep and covered in the same faded red and green carpet. Dinah takes them two at a time.

He calls after her, 'And some underwear.' Dinah nearly misses a step and stumbles.

The room smells stale, fusty and sour. The bed is a mess. Dinah doesn't really want to go in but she has to. Two thin, flowery curtains are half open and a dirty light sifts through the small, low windows. She didn't realise how bad the house had become since he's been living alone. She feels sorry for him all of a sudden.

Dinah's mother used to clean the farmhouse, she used to bring his washing down to the cottage and put it in with theirs, iron it afterwards. Once or twice, Dinah had to take it back up to the farmhouse and leave it in a black plastic bag outside the door. She would see him sometimes, at the same kitchen table with a screwdriver or a hammer or bent over a plate eating bread like a starving man.

But then the laundry stopped and instead Dinah's mother became 'Anne O'Neill, Virtual PA', doing all Ahab's ordering online, stuff for the van repairs, paying bills, all his accounts, answering the phone, anything and everything that involves the outside world.

But all the same, he should open a window occasionally, pick all his clothes up, change the duvet cover, put things away. Vacuum once in a while. He doesn't care about himself and he doesn't care about anyone else either.

There's a pile of clothes on a chair. Dinah grabs a few things and then gingerly picks up two pairs of boxer shorts. They look clean but who knows. Dinah has lived on her own with her mother for years and years. There's no man in the house, no boys, not even visitors. She'd been all alone stuck out in the middle of nowhere and then finally she got to go to school and what does she do? Ruins everything. Breaks her world apart. Typical Dinah.

She bundles everything up in a bedspread and brings them downstairs.

'My coat,' he says, gesturing to a peg on the back door.

Dinah watches him pull a hat over his hair, still mud-caked.

'I need a piss,' he mutters.

Dinah shudders at the word and the way he speaks. He makes her feel sick, the way he smells, the way he shouts. She walks backwards towards the door. 'I'm going to get my stuff,' she says and runs down the track back home. Everything's still there waiting, obviously. No one comes this far up the lane. She picks up her bags . . . but wait.

She doesn't have to go back. She didn't promise anything. She could just take off across the fields; she'd be gone in a moment and Ahab wouldn't have a chance of catching her. Not with one leg and a broom for a crutch. But he is going south at least. And she'd get four hundred quid. And she wouldn't have to hitchhike.

By the time she walks back up the hill, he's locked his front door and is waiting on the top step. 'Where are you going with that lot?' he says, gesturing to her holdall. 'Two days at the very most. One, if you drive like you mean it.'

Dinah says nothing. She doesn't have to answer. She just stands so he can lean on her shoulder as he hops down, one, pause, two, pause, three. He's heavy and she groans under the weight.

'You should get some muscles on you, girl. All you lot do is play on your phones all the bloody time. I tried to get me an apprentice a few years back. Did anyone apply? One half-witted little runt the size of a badger. Ran off after I asked him a few questions. Couldn't look me in the eye. Told the woman at the Job Centre not to send me any more narrowbacks. So I do it all myself.'

They shuffle over to the barn and Dinah pulls the door open. She hasn't seen inside since she was a child. It was different then. There was an old, green caravan with no door with all the stuffing ripped out of the seats. Dinah and the other children used to climb inside and play house, long summers jumping on and off the rickety table watching spiders spin their cotton wool traps. The whole place was a mess then with nooks and crannies for hide-and-seek, with nests in corners where wild cats hissed and scratched and birds swooped down from the rafters. And there was a massive, wide brown American car that somehow took six adults and five children with room to spare.

Dinah's not just leaving home, she's leaving New Bedford and everything it stood for, all of those memories, all of the things she grew up with. But it's too late now.

2. Dinah

At the New Bedford Fellowship, everyone agreed that Dinah's mother was the Mother of the commune. People even called her Saint Anne or Mother Anne though she wasn't the oldest person by a long way. She was calm and wise and people used to ask to see her so they could talk about their problems and she would always give people her time when they needed her.

Once, when she was about seven, Dinah was with her mother in the Prayer Yurt. They were supposed to be in Silent Time but Dinah couldn't keep still. Her mother was sitting on a cushion with her eyes closed and Dinah was supposed to be doing the same. But the rough carpet was itchy and the yurt was a bit too hot and Dinah was thirsty and she'd been in lessons with her mother all day trying to learn maths and now she had to sit still. Anne opened one eye and looked at her.

'Silent Time, Dinah. You know what that means. Five minutes. Sit still and think about something. Anything – but something peaceful, something quiet.'

Anne closed her eye and Dinah sat on her hands. Then she scratched her leg. Then she looked up to the ceiling at the wooden struts that kept the yurt together. Then there was a daddy longlegs on the wall. Then there was a hole in her jumper and when you pulled the thread the hole got bigger. Then Anne opened one eye again and then the other.

'Come,' she said and Dinah sat on her lap. 'What is it?'

'I want to be big.'

'Why?'

'Because Jonah keeps telling me he's bigger than me.'

'He is.'

'And I want to be strong.'

'You are strong, Dinah.'

'I know but Jonah's bigger and he won't let me play with him.'

'He's strong and big in the way that boys are. You are strong and big in the way that girls are, in the way that women are.'

'I don't like him. He runs too fast and I can't catch him. And he does things without me and won't tell me.'

'Dinah, he's your friend, my love. Come.'

Dinah snuggled into her mother. She loved the smell of her jumpers and her scarves, of the oils she rubbed into her skin, of the flowers she wore in her hair.

'Tell me the story about Our Beginning,' said Dinah.

Anne sighed. 'All right. But then you have to sit quietly, OK?'

'I promise.'

'Well, before the Fellowship I was wandering the earth looking for a place of peace.'

'Where did you live?'

'Oh, different parts of Ireland, then Spain, lots of different countries, Canada, Holland, France, meeting lots of different people.'

'Who did you meet?'

'Lots of people, good people mostly, some bad people as well but I didn't spend any time with them. I stuck to the nice people that wanted to live a good life and learn about the spirit. I made lots of friends, lots of sisters and brothers, and your father was one of them. He had also been wandering all over the earth, looking for a place of peace, so we got married.'

'I wasn't born, was I?'

'No. But we thought about having you so we decided to get married. But we didn't want a wedding with a white dress and a priest. So we found a holy place and we bound our hands together with leaves. We sang songs and we said what we wanted from our lives and how we would always live together in truth and in love. And our hands stayed bound together for the whole day and the whole night then the next morning when the leaves dropped off, that's it, we were married.'

'Then me.'

'Yes, then you. And before you were born we had to choose a name so we decided to call you Dinah if you were a girl, which you were. And Dinah means The Wise One. That's you.'

'With my big heart.'

'With your big heart, yes.'

'And my big hair?'

'And your beautiful, black hair, yes.'

'What if I was a boy?'

'If you were a boy you would be Ishmael.'

'Ishmael. I like that name.'

'It's a good name, Dinah. It means The Good Listener. So really it means that you have to listen to what your heart says and for that you have to be quiet.'

'I want Ishmael for my second name.'

'All right then. Ishmael it is.'

'What happened then?'

'Dinah, Tego and Anne lived all over the place in different communes and retreats and on our own in the woods and in a different Fellowship in Scotland but when they heard about New Bedford they knew they had found the right place to live for the rest of their lives.'

'And we'll be here for ever.'

Anne kissed her on her head. 'Yes, lovely girl. But now, sit there. Silent Time, my love.'

3. Dinah

Dinah stands next to Ahab and stares in at the mess. Loads of vehicles are scattered about the barn, all of them Volkswagen campervans; some are dead, some are dying, some have no wheels, no roof, no sides, two are beautiful, one red, one blue. Spare parts hang from the ceiling, a pyramid of rusty metal obliterates the huge back doors, one wall is given over to tools of every description lined up neatly on a grid, and machines and gauges and coils and wires are everywhere like it's a factory for a dozen workers.

Ahab stands for a moment, the broom wobbling under his arm, and looks around. He hops to the red VW and runs his hand along its flank.

'Ah, Cromarty Jane, you're a good girl,' he says. 'But you're delicate. Never been happy with those gear ratios. Don't know how a stranger will treat you and I can't risk it.' His voice is different, soft and low.

He looks at Dinah and winks. 'Now, him. He's the man for the job.' He points at the blue van. 'Put your stuff in the back. And be careful with him. I would have liked another couple of weeks on that engine but there you go. No time now. We need to catch the bastard that stole my van. Come on, don't hang about. We need to catch them. Hurry up.'

Ahab caresses the side of the campervan like it's alive, like it's his favourite dog. 'He's a '73 T2 Westfalia. And you don't get many of them to the dollar. Get in. Go on.'

Dinah slides the side door open. It's a smooth easy movement. The floor is tiled in black and white like a doll's kitchen, with a little wooden table and built-in seats. There are cotton curtains of blue and white check and slender cupboards in every corner. It smells of leather and polish and it all looks new.

'Wow,' she says. 'It's nice.'

He's next to her in a second, leaning on the side of the van. 'Nice? Took me four bloody years. Nice doesn't come close.' He mutters all the way into the passenger seat. 'Nice, my arse.' The soft, petting voice is gone. The bully is back.

As soon as she sits in the driver's seat, Ahab starts pointing everything out and telling her about the clutch and the dials and the gear stick and on and on until they've been sitting there for fifteen minutes.

Dinah sighs. 'All right, all right,' she says. 'I've got it.'

'Him.'

'Him?'

'Yes, him. The Pequod. That's his name. When something means something to you, you name it. Something with no name means nobody cares about it, nobody took enough trouble to get to know it, how it works, what's underneath. Vans should have the perfect name, just like people.'

Dinah almost envied The Pequod and its perfect name. Her own name sounded old-fashioned, outdated, like someone who had lived in a commune her whole life.

4. Dinah

Childhood was magical at the New Bedford Fellowship. There was a motto that all the children had to learn. 'Love in Truth. Worship in Freedom. All in One Spirit.'

In summer all the gatherings were outside under the big oak tree and in winter the prayers were in the farmhouse drawing room. The first half was silent prayer and the second half was Exhortation when someone would say something nice to everyone else about the way they felt about God or Christ or Buddha or Allah or Jehovah or The Great Mother or whatever they wanted to call The Spirit. Then after everyone said, 'So be it,' all the children had a story and could go out to play, which was the best time of all.

When someone wanted to moan or if there were arguments, everyone sat in the Truth Circle and the person that wanted to speak sat in the middle and said anything they liked. Everyone had to listen and no one could answer back, not even the person that was being accused. Then the next day, the person that was supposed to have done something wrong could sit in the middle if they wanted to and have their say but nearly every time they didn't and everyone said sorry and it was over and done with.

But because he owned the land and the farmhouse, Ahab would sit in the middle more often than anyone else and he'd whinge and moan and make speeches for so long that the children would fall asleep. Once Dinah heard someone call the Truth Circle 'Ahab's Ring' and everyone burst out laughing.

Even though it's impossible, all the days seem like they were sunny except for Christmas when it was snowy with icicles hanging off the roof and fairy lights around the windows. There was honey cake and treacle scones and sometimes it was too cold to play outside.

And on those days, Dinah's family would go up to the farmhouse more often. The two families were very close. When they were younger, Jonah and Dinah would go up to his room and play with his wooden animals or look through his telescope at the stars. Jonah used to paint metal cars and sometimes both of them would have a race. Jonah always won because he was three years older and cleverer but Dinah didn't mind because he was her best friend and she loved him like he loved her. There were just the two of them more often than not, just those two together for hours and hours, talking and playing and making up games.

All the families had a story, how they didn't believe in organised religion or they had been kicked out of their congregation for not keeping the rules or they wanted to join a community of free thinkers. Ahab and Caroline were both brought up in a strict religion where men couldn't have beards and women had to know their place. They all had to marry someone else in the congregation or the elders would tell them off.

No one was surprised that Ahab couldn't keep the rules. He was still always asking questions and always thinking about the way things were done and Caroline said that people either loved Ahab or avoided Ahab.

But what Dinah remembers most of all before the Fellowship fell apart was love and games and holding hands and being safe. It was the whole world. Good, kind people from all corners of the earth living together at the farmhouse, in the farm cottages, in tents, in caravans, in outbuildings, so many different voices and accents and five children of all ages but Dinah was the second oldest just behind Jonah. Then all the other kids were babies and toddlers, too young for Jonah and Dinah to play with.

Other people used to come as well, visitors and teachers for weekends who would camp or stay with Ahab, Caroline and Jonah.

Caroline didn't look old enough to be Jonah's mum. She didn't look old enough to be Ahab's wife either. She had long, brown hair that she always had in two plaits coiled like a wreath around her head or covered over in a silk scarf in purple or blue that matched her eyes and the jewellery she made. She wore long dresses with tassels and fringes and was always singing and humming to herself, always making potions and medicines from betony, prunella, feverfew, all the plants and flowers that grew around the Fellowship.

Apart from Dinah's mum, Caroline was the nicest of all the New Bedford women. Dinah loved her. She was the one with all the best stories at the gatherings, the one who took the children into the wood to teach them about nature. All of Caroline's lessons felt more like playtime and then, before you knew it, you'd done something you'd never done before and learnt something really good.

There were always gatherings and picnics and Silent Time and the Prayer Yurt, and in the woods near the Golden Lake there was a fire pit for barbecues and burning things. People used to burn secrets or letters to The Spirit or things that needed to stay unsaid or prayers or nice things that you wanted to say to someone that had died or someone that couldn't come to the Fellowship.

Once, Dinah burnt a nice poem that she sent to her grandmother in heaven and once, just before Dinah's dad left he burnt something in the fire and Dinah's mother started crying. Dinah was only twelve then but she remembers that there had been arguments at home, quiet arguments but arguments all the same, different words she'd never heard before said in different voices even though both voices belonged to her parents. They thought she was asleep. They thought she couldn't understand and the truth was she didn't but even when the arguing was silent, she knew that something had changed. She began to feel sick when she went to bed. She began to have nightmares or bad dreams. She began to wonder what was wrong because everyone was quiet but there was noise in the air just the same, all unspoken things between her parents and between other people in the Fellowship. Just because people weren't speaking it didn't mean things weren't being said.

5. Dinah

The rain starts again, drumming on the metal roof of the garage. The potholed track will be treacherous. A long, long drive with a one-legged man, hours and days with him, swearing and shouting at her all the way. All of a sudden Dinah is breathless. She can't do it. Her hands begin to shake and she can't swallow.

'What are you waiting for?' he says.

Dinah turns the key and The Pequod purrs into life.

'Good lad,' says Ahab, slapping the dashboard. 'Off we sail.'

The manoeuvre from garage to track is tricky. Dinah tries to remember what her driving instructor said about reversing and getting out of difficult parking places. Actually, he hasn't covered either of those yet because Dinah is only on her fourth driving lesson and her test isn't even booked in. 'Be a confident road user,' the instructor always says. 'Too slow is as dangerous as too fast.'

She threads the steering wheel through her hands as best she can but feels the sweat prickle under her arms, feels the tremors in her legs. If she crashes, he'll know she's still learning and then she won't get paid. It all feels like a massive mistake.

Somehow she does it. She puts her foot down and it just happens. They are driving along Tanners Lane in two minutes. She wants to shout and laugh out loud but Dinah can feel Ahab's eyes on her the whole time. She keeps checking all the mirrors, back, front and sides, and she keeps the van at thirty miles per hour but really she doesn't have to remember a thing because Ahab won't shut up.

'Easy. Clutch out. Gentle. Don't over-rev him. Take him wide here. Easy, girl. Give him some juice.'

She's driving, really driving a proper vehicle. Maybe if Queenie could see her now, in charge, all on her own, in control of something so beautiful, being someone completely different. If Queenie could see her then . . . But it's too late for ifs and buts after what Dinah has done.

But she can't help it. One by one, Dinah thinks of all Queenie's faces, the one where she's concentrating at her desk, when her lips go slack and her eyelids nearly close, her black lashes against her white skin. Then the face of laughter when someone says something funny in class but no one can make a sound, when Dinah catches her eye, when the smile stretches across Queenie's face and she's trying to keep the laughter inside. But the best of all Queenie's faces is the one that's serious, up close, listening like Dinah is the only person in the world, like there's just the two of them, always. But that's all ruined now. And Dinah did it all on her own.

There's nothing for it but to disappear. If she's far enough away then maybe when she thinks about Queenie, maybe, one day, eventually, some time in the future, her heart won't feel like it's about to break. She won't feel her face go hot and red; she won't feel like her world is about to end. She needs to put distance between herself and the scene of her crime.

Ahab points to a sign. 'A1. We can pick it up in five miles. Takes us straight to the motorway. Go right.'

He kneads the nub of his knee as he speaks and sucks the air in through his teeth. 'Killing me, this leg. The cold. The damp. This bloody northern wind.'

Dinah glances at him. 'Haven't you got a spare?'

'A spare leg?'

'A false one?'

'Have I got a spare false leg?'

'I thought . . .'

'What? That the National Health Service make you a couple of legs at a time in case someone runs off with one?'

Dinah nearly smiles.

6. Dinah

She'd had to fight her mother every step of the way. All the homeschooled kids sat their exams at different times and Dinah had got brilliant results in hers. Dinah's mother kept saying how well she'd done and how they could now start the A level curriculum together. But Dinah had other ideas.

'I want to go to Kingsley High School, Mum.'

'You know how I feel about schools, Dinah.'

'I really want to go. I'll do my A levels there.'

'You'll do better at home with me. I hear things about that school.'

'I just want to see what it's like. Everyone goes there.' Wrong thing to say, Dinah. 'Everyone' was exactly the wrong thing to say.

'Like who?'

'I mean the other kids from round here and some of the homeschoolers.'

It went like that for weeks and weeks. With Dinah asking and begging and her mother saying no without actually saying no.

'We came here to get away from the "everyone does it" mentality, Dinah. Just because everyone does something doesn't mean we have to. There are drugs at school, teenage pregnancies, an overreliance on technology and easy answers. We believe in doing things differently, don't we? Don't we?'

In her heart Dinah always said the same thing: 'No, we don't!' Upstairs in her room she would sit against the door in case her mum tried to come in and carry on where she left off. There was a world out there somewhere, a world of excitement and friendships and people that would understand her. All the best years of her life were turning to grey dust and blowing away in the wind and there was nothing she could do about it. Unless she ran away. But where would she go? And how would she get there? And really was she brave enough, crazy enough?

Ahab would never know he was the turning point, he was the one who changed Anne's mind. It was the middle of July. Dinah and her mother were in their little front garden. Dinah was lying on the grass with her workbook over her face. It had taken her a whole hour to do five impossible, unworkable equations. And the answers were wrong.

Definitely. All Dinah could hear was the flies, the bees, the wasps, the sounds of a hot summer's day, and inside she was rehearsing yet another bout of pleading that she be allowed to go to school. She needed a new argument, a new angle of attack.

Then voices. Hardly any visitors came up the track apart from the postman and people that were lost but someone was calling. 'Hello? Hello?'

Dinah and her mother went to the gate. There were two women there, about the same age as Anne, walkers in boots and backpacks. 'I'm sorry, we're lost,' said the first woman, pulling out a map. 'Is this the Brandon Way?'

'No, no,' said Anne. 'You're a good way west of that.'

'Yes, I thought so,' the woman replied. She looked flustered, upset and tired, and Dinah's mum offered them a cup of tea.

'No, we'll get off,' she said. 'We've just had a rather nasty experience with the man up there. He shouted at us, told us to get off his property. Said we were trespassing. Rude.'

'He lives alone up there,' said Anne. 'He doesn't get many visitors, I'm afraid. He's not very sociable.'

'Explains everything,' said the woman. 'What can you expect? Isolation makes people strange.'

'Very unhealthy,' said the other.

Then they were gone. Dinah thought nothing of it but that night her mother sat on the end of her bed.

'You don't feel isolated here, do you, Dinah?'

'A bit.' She wanted to say a lot, she wanted to scream and say, 'Yes! I hate it here!' but she knew that if she wanted her own way she had to act better than that.

'You don't feel strange or different? I mean to other children.'

'A bit.'

'Well, you have the Virtual School, don't you? And the Homeschool Network.'

'Once a month, Mum?'

'Maybe you wouldn't like school?'

'I would.' She wouldn't say any more. If she wanted her own way, Dinah would have to take it slow this time.

Then the next day, Ahab came down to the cottage to bring a list of things he wanted. Dinah heard her mother talking to him at the front door.

'You upset those two women yesterday, Ahab.'

'So? And I need all that stuff by next week.'

'You should get out more.'

'Said the party animal.' He walked away and stopped at the gate. 'You're just as antisocial as I am, Anne, in case you hadn't noticed. We're not so different, if you ask me. You and that girl stuck up here all day. Pot calling the kettle black.'

The same evening, Dinah's mother told her she could go to school. 'You've got your life ahead of you. We'll give it a try but if I think it's not good for you . . .'

That night, Dinah turned over in bed and smiled into the blackness.

7. Ishmael

Driving on the A1 isn't like driving on Tanners Lane. It's a different beast altogether. Cars speed past, so close to the van that it's hard to hold it straight. Motorbikes slalom through the traffic, pulling in front of The Pequod and then tearing off again. Out of the blue, the road curves back on itself then dips and rises without warning. Dinah presses the brake too hard and the whole van jerks and shudders. She might crash. She might kill them both.

What was she doing? She'd let Ahab bully her into committing another crime but this wasn't the time to think about it. She has to concentrate. Hard.

Suddenly, Dinah finds herself in the slipstream of a juggernaut that churns the wind and obliterates the sky. She tries to remember all the things her driving instructor told her but it's no good. There are cars slipping in front and behind, so close she can see the driver in her mirror. Lorries thunder past on the other side of the road, monster trucks with tyres a metre and a half high; shiny new cars race past in a blur and all the time there is Ahab next to her, watching her learner's mistakes. She feels sick with fright.

'Pull off,' he says. 'Come off! Now! Take the next road on the left.'

Dinah turns the steering wheel, slowly leaves the main road and pulls over into a side road.

'You lied,' says Ahab, leaning over and taking the keys out of the ignition.

Dinah won't cry because that's what he wants.

'You haven't passed your bloody test, have you?'

Dinah shakes her head. 'I didn't lie. I just didn't answer you.'

'Same difference.'

'It isn't,' she whispers but really she wants to shout and tell him to leave her alone. Shout at him like he shouts at everyone else. See how he likes it.

She turns away and stares out of the window. It's not like she's innocent. It's not like she's done nothing wrong. She's ruined everything.

Ahab rubs his face with both hands. 'Christ, we're going to have to go back.'

'No!' That's the last thing Dinah wants. Going back isn't an option. She's left now, on her way, she's never going back, never.

'Look,' she says to Ahab. 'Do you want me to drive or not? You can't do it, can you, with one leg?'

'This isn't a joke, Dinah, I–'

'I'm not Dinah.'

'What?'

'I'm not Dinah any more.'

Ahab raises his eyebrows. 'Since when?'

'Since this morning.'

She pulls the woollen hat off her head and shows him her baldness. All in all, it took her an hour to get rid of it all, her crowning glory as her mother called it or her Girlie Curls as Queenie once said. It would never trail down her back again, no more purple-black waves, heavy and sleek as the midnight sea. She thinks of it coiled in the bottom of her bag. Thinks of what her mum would say if she saw the pale baldness, the nicks and scratches she made by mistake. It still feels new, sore in places, tender.

She had lain in bed all night, watched the sun come up, watched the fields turn from black to green and the sky turn grey, then white, then grey again. Dinah's arms had ached by the time she'd finished but oh the look of her, the person in the mirror, that was worth the pain. She was fierce and strong, she looked like a different person. A person who didn't make mistakes. A person who could get on with her life, far away. A person who might look nineteen or twenty,

41

who could get a job and start again with no bad history and no shame following her around.

The small cuts where the blades had caught her skin just added to the look. People would think she had been in a fight, a hard girl from a hard place. No one would laugh at her ever again. She turns from right to left so Ahab can see.

'Right,' says Ahab, staring at her head. 'You look like a bloody convict. Who are you now, then?'

Dinah snatches the key out of his hand and feeds it in the ignition. The Pequod coughs into life. Over the sound of the engine, Dinah shouts it out.

'Call me Ishmael.'

8. Dinah

It was September, Dinah's very first day of school and she was sixteen years old. It was too hot for shoes so she wore flip flops. Her mum dropped her outside on her first day.

'The school bus will pick you up here at four o'clock, OK, Dinah? It drops you where I showed you. You'll be fine.'

Dinah couldn't wait for her mother to drive away. She didn't want the whole school watching her mother give her instructions on where to go and what do.

'Just go, Mum. Quick.'

Dinah walked through the gates and into the playground. It was enormous, acres of concrete, hundreds of kids, and no one spoke to her. Everyone knew everyone else, there were groups of kids laughing and joking, but Dinah didn't even know where to stand.

And she'd spent so long at the commune she didn't even know what the right clothes were. There was no uniform but all the girls wore the same thing, tight jeans and tight T-shirts that showed their shape, some that didn't even cover their stomachs, some with glitter and stuff written on them, some with rips and zips and tears. And all the boys did the same, hoodies and T-shirts and low-slung jeans or jeans so tight they could hardly sit down, and special kinds of trainers in canvas and leather. Dinah knew she was staring but she couldn't help it and anyway she wanted to memorise everything so she could buy the right stuff and not look so out of place.

Everyone was looking at their phones or taking photographs but Dinah's mother disagreed with smartphones. Dinah's tiny black phone could only make calls and texts and compared to the mini-computers all the other kids had, hers looked ugly and useless like something from ancient history. She couldn't even get it out without drawing attention to herself.

At least her rucksack looked all right because Dinah had bought it herself with her own money. Inside, she had pens and paper but she wasn't sure what else to bring. She had five pounds in her pocket but she didn't know if that was too much or not enough or whether she would need any money at all.

That day seemed to last for ever. She was mostly on her own, reading a timetable she could barely understand, sitting at the back of the class with boys who stared at her and girls who ignored her. And when they weren't ignoring her, they were asking her the same questions.

'What does it even mean to be homeschooled?'

'Did you even have any proper lessons?'

'So is that why you haven't got any friends?'

And then there was the day Dinah heard her teacher talking to the head of the school.

'Who's taught her, I simply don't know. She's head and shoulders above most of the others academically but quite strange, as you would expect.'

Strange. Dinah felt ashamed but it was true. She didn't know where to sit or how to use the lockers or what the other kids were saying half the time; she didn't know all the TV programmes they watched, the names of the bands they listened to; she didn't know what the best shops were or where people went after school. Everything about the other kids left her on the outside and the girls' clothes and make-up made her feel dull and out of date.

In the sixth form common room, there were only two conversations. Layla and the other kids talked about the sports teacher Mr Oakfield who had left suddenly last year.

'He's a paedo,' they said. 'He was going out with Amber from 5K and she's like fifteen. I mean, she was actually having sex with him.'

Layla made vomit signs with her hands. 'He's like forty or something.'

The girl had left the school and Mr Oakfield had been arrested. All the kids had been interviewed by the police and asked if he'd done anything else to them, assaulted them or said anything wrong.

'He'll go to prison,' everyone said. 'He's a pervert.'

And if it wasn't Mr Oakfield and Amber, the other conversation was about contouring make-up, about eyeliner and highlighter, stuff that Dinah had never even seen let alone used. Nearly everyone used straighteners on their hair; they'd plug them in at lunchtime and groom each other with sprays and lotions that made the room smell like a beauty salon. Not that Dinah had ever even been into a beauty salon but she imagined the endless brushing and squirting that went on. Once, when Dinah was watching out of the corner of her eye, one of the girls pointed at Dinah's hair.

'The only good thing about you is that lot,' the girl said. 'I mean it's like really long and thick and those massive curls and stuff. Is that natural? Wish I had that lot but honestly, do something with it, you'd look a lot better.'

She was trying to be nice.

'And your eyebrows are like . . . like really weird,' said another. 'Get them waxed. Or threaded or something.' Dinah had never even heard of something being threaded. What did it mean? Everyone stared at her, waiting for an answer, but she didn't know what to say.

9. Ishmael

Then they're off again. There's a slower road south, narrow and curling, and it weaves between the hillside villages, between the farms and cottages, past the disused mine and abandoned railway stations. It looks bleak and dark and Ishmael can't imagine living there.

'These places were dead before you were alive,' says Ahab, pointing every so often.

He shakes his head. 'That's why we chose this area. Land was dirt cheap, houses as well. I bought the whole place for a song. The house, the land, the cottages, the lake. We thought we were clever. Sold up, lock, stock and barrel. London prices. Sold everything and just came up here. Put the word out that we were making something special. Holy Island over there, the land of God. We all had imaginations then, optimism. Every Sunday afternoon all sitting together in the farmhouse. Remember? Kids running up and down all over the place, you and Jonah ... your mum with storytime in front of the fire. Big roast dinners, big talk, big ideas. Big nothing in the end. Bloody idiots we were. Everyone except your mother.'

Ahab sounds like he's talking to himself. Remembering and talking slowly with pain in his voice. But Ishmael remembers as well.

It's Dinah's birthday. She's thirteen and if she didn't know better she would think she was catching up with Jonah. She's getting taller by the day. Jonah might be fifteen but he's not that tall and Dinah's nearly past his shoulders.

According to the rules at the New Bedford Fellowship, when it's someone's birthday, they're in charge of everything and everyone. You can eat what you like, do what you like, ask someone to play with you or take you somewhere and they have to obey. Dinah is the boss for the whole day.

She's already had pancakes for breakfast with honey from the hives. She's opened all of her presents: potions and lotions, and pens and a leather bag that her father made which is beautiful and must have taken him ages. There are things for her hair, oils and combs, and Caroline has painted a picture of her with all her hair in waves like a mermaid. Her mother has made a necklace of shells from the beach at Scremerston and bought her book after book after book. And Jonah? He's made her a packet of handmade paper. He tied the bundle with a rope of plaited ivy and wrapped it in a silk scarf. Dinah knows that his mum must have helped him but the idea is all his. It's their secret.

It all started when they were in Silent Time. The adults can't get enough of it, all sitting on the floor in the Prayer Yurt in absolute silence. Sometimes, if there is no wind and no rain you can actually hear people breathing and when it's that quiet it always makes Dinah want to laugh. She thinks of something and because she can't make a sound, that's all she wants to do. Shuffling, coughing, moving position, sighing – any single movement makes a noise and Dinah cannot stand it. Neither can Jonah.

Jonah started the game. It was Tego's turn to lead the meditation. He was sitting cross-legged at the front of the group with his hands together. He spoke slowly in his most serious and spiritual voice.

'We are here in this moment. We come into our bodies, come into our minds. We are alone. We are together. We are open. We are still.'

Then he rang a little bell. *Ping.* Slowly, everyone nodded and closed their eyes. This was the time when everyone was supposed to be mindful, to be thinking of nothing. But for Dinah it was long, drawn-out and painful. How could you think of nothing? What did that even mean? If you were thinking of nothing you were still thinking, and anyway after five seconds you'd think about your breathing or what you did yesterday and then immediately, you had broken the rules.

Then after five minutes, Dinah felt something move under her knee. Carefully and almost invisibly she slipped her hand down to her leg, centimetre by centimetre, and felt a piece of paper folded up so many times it was no bigger than a nut. She opened her eyes a tiny fraction and scanned the room. Everyone was meditating. She dropped her hands into the hidden space in her crossed legs and with her very fingertips she opened the note.

'Sandra likes honey.' That's all it said.

It was Jonah's handwriting but Jonah was sitting perfectly still with his eyes closed and his hands in his lap.

Dinah knew that if she wanted to see Sandra she would have to turn round and moving was dangerous. It made a noise. But she had to do it. She scanned the room again. No one was looking. As quietly as she could, Dinah twisted her neck and looked behind her. There was Sandra, normally so quiet and reserved, the big-cheeked woman who was in charge of the kitchen and the communal food stores who had decided today to tie her hair into two massive brown knots on top of her head exactly like bear's ears. 'Sandra likes honey.'

Before Dinah knew it, the giggle had begun. It started in her chest and worked its way north until it was in her throat. Her eyes began to water and she bit the inside of her cheek. She mustn't laugh. But then she let out a squeak, then a chortle, and before she knew it the laughter was out, loud and free, and there was nothing she could do about it. Her father opened his eyes and shook his head but the giggle had started and couldn't be recalled. Helpless, she looked at Jonah and only she could see the slightest wrinkle at the corners of his lips, to everyone else he was still in meditation.

Her father asked her to take the noise outside so she did and afterwards, when the meditation was over, Dinah's mother and father told her they were disappointed and that her laughter had disturbed the others, and even though Dinah had to have another Silent Time on her own that evening, it had been worth it. The game had started. The challenge was set. She had to break Jonah down and make him laugh.

She began to look forward to Silent Time. She would spend her days trying to overhear what the adults were saying in case there were any jokes, she would watch the younger children in case they did anything funny. And then she would pass him a note in Silent Time, or in lessons, or late at night she would find one slipped into her pocket some time during the day. Jonah was always the best. She could make him smile but he would make her collapse into giggles she couldn't control. Even when they could talk freely about ordinary things, they preferred notes.

So Jonah's handmade paper for her birthday present is like another secret between them and it's the best thing ever. She cuts one piece of paper in half, writes 'Golden Lake' on it and walks up to the farmhouse. Jonah and his father are standing by the barn mending one of the vans. She walks over, pops the note in the back of Jonah's jeans and sits on the back step of the farmhouse to wait.

The Golden Lake is the calmest and prettiest place in the whole of New Bedford. When it was sunny and bright, the lake looked green and silver with the leaves reflected on the flat surface of the water. Sometimes, birds would balance on bits of wood or swoop down and pluck things out of the lake and fly off again. But in the autumn when the leaves turned yellow and orange, the lake became a bowl of fire, golden and shimmering like it was alive, warm and breathing, a sleeping lion.

It's not like Jonah to take a long time to answer.

She goes back to the barn and stands where Jonah can see her. She stands there and stands there and eventually he steps away from the van and whispers, 'No.'

'It's my birthday, Jonah. You have to.'

'We can go tomorrow,' he says. 'Not now.' Then he walks back to his father, back to Ahab banging metal on metal, the sound clanging like a gong, like a warning about something.

Dinah's cheeks blush hot and red. She might be growing up but it's Jonah who's changing. He doesn't want her around.

10. Ishmael

It's four o'clock. They're driving through ribbons of villages with little shops huddled along the pavement, butchers and newsagents, closed down post offices and banks. From time to time, Ahab clutches the nub of his knee in his big hand, holds it, strokes it and sometimes hits it with his palm as though he's telling it off, like it's done something wrong.

They haven't passed a café or service station for hours. They haven't passed a shop or a garage either. Ishmael remembers her sandwiches.

'Can you pass me that carrier bag?' she says.

'Why?' says Ahab. 'You're not checking your phone while you're driving, if that's what you're thinking. All you lot ever do is—'

'I haven't got a phone any more,' says Ishmael.

'Good.'

'I just want food,' Ishmael says. 'Sandwiches. That's what's in the bag.'

Ahab leans back and grabs the bag. He puts it on his lap and rubs his hands together. 'Let's see what we've got here. If God is good, we'll have a couple of ham rolls or cheese and pickle on granary. Crisps would be taking providence too far. Flapjack? Nah. Too much to hope for at this juncture.'

But what Ahab takes out of the bag is not what Ishmael put in. Somehow, the sandwiches, the white bread, the cheese and the jam, have all merged together into a red, sticky mess, damp crusts hanging off an oozing flat, red and yellow pancake.

'What the hell is this?'

'Oh no, it's all squashed,' Ishmael says smiling at the disgust on his face. 'Kitchen roadkill.'

Ahab holds it up to the light. 'It's supposed to look like this *after* you've eaten it. Not before.' He slops it back into the carrier bag. 'Anything else in here?'

'The milk should be all right,' she says.

'Milk? I'm forty-five years old not forty-five days. Milk? I don't think so. What else?' He peers into the bag and carefully extracts the packet of biscuits. 'Zesty Lemon Crunch with a Lemon & Lime Cream Centre. Merridew's Economy Range.' He drops them like they're poisonous.

Ishmael puts her hand out. 'I'll have one.'

Ahab ties the carrier bag handles together and throws the whole thing out of the window. 'Not in my van, you won't.'

'I thought littering was against the law,' she says.

'Yeah, like driving without a licence. So we're both criminals. Take the next right.'

They pull into a small garage with only one petrol pump. An old woman with a puff of grey hair sits with her arms folded behind a counter in a small scruffy shack. She saunters out when she sees The Pequod and grabs the nozzle of the pump. She eyes Ahab and then Ishmael, then Ahab again.

'Here he is,' she says through the window of the van. 'The campervan man.'

'Fill her up,' says Ahab and takes some money out of his pocket.

'Well, now, that van we bought off you was done right, and I don't say that often,' says the woman, feeding the petrol nozzle into the side of the van. 'My husband's out now taking a drive, bless him. Best work he's ever seen, he says. You did it perfect. So perfect, I never get a go in it.'

'Do you sell sandwiches in there?' says Ahab, pointing at the shack.

'Go on in,' she says. 'You have a look.'

Ishmael helps Ahab shuffle over to the hut. There is a small display fridge with rolls and sandwiches of dark brown bread. There is a row of sticky doughnuts on the top shelf with sprinkles of hundreds and thousands. Ishmael takes enough for both of them even though the whole place smells of cigarettes and damp. Then she adds two bottles of water and a packet of crisps.

The woman finishes with the petrol and walks back into the shack. She stares at Ishmael. 'This your daughter?'

Ahab hands some money over. She puts all their food in a cardboard box and shoves it across the counter. 'Didn't know you had kids. Your wife not with you? Where you off to? Holidays? You still doing the vans? That's a nice one. Is it for sale? You managing all right with that leg?'

'No, she isn't,' says Ahab. 'And none of your business to the rest of your bloody questions.' He grabs the box and gives it to Ishmael. He takes his change and puts his hand on Ishmael's shoulder. 'Go,' he says.

'Well I never!' says the woman as they both hurry out of the shop.

Ishmael drives off immediately, too embarrassed to wave at the woman, who is now standing with her hands on her hips at the door of the hut.

After ten minutes, they pull into a side road. Ahab takes a sandwich out of the box. 'Pastrami on rye,' he says, looking closely at it. 'Mustard and pickle. Not bad for an old bag.'

'Why are you so rude to everyone?'

'I know that woman. Nosy old witch. I don't like pity, and you might like answering personal questions,' he says, passing Ishmael a sandwich, 'but I don't.'

They eat in silence. Ishmael finishes her sandwich and starts on the doughnut which has sweet, thick cream inside and a dusting of icing sugar. She still looks like a little girl, even without the hair. She needs to look older, like someone who can take care of herself. She needs to find a job and a flat and be self-sufficient. She has an old hoodie in her bag. She reaches behind and pulls her bag forward. She finds the hoodie and puts it on. No one would recognise her in that. If her mum calls the police when she finds out she's missing, they'll be looking for a young girl with a mane of hair not a bald woman in a hoodie.

She's still starving when the sandwich is finished.

'Take it,' says Ahab, offering her a second one. He watches her take the first bite. 'Jonah used to have a sweet tooth,' he says. 'Even when he was a baby. We used to put honey on his fingers. We used to—' Ahab stops abruptly, like he realises what he's saying, like it's a secret.

'He still does,' says Ishmael. 'Last time I saw him we went for a pizza. He had—'

'Never mind that,' he interrupts. 'I don't care. I don't want to talk about it. And anyway, if you're so keen to answer questions, you can tell me where you were going.'

'When?'

'When I knocked on the door. You were just about to leave. And you had a bag already packed. Where were you going?'

Ishmael pops the last bit of doughnut in her mouth and wipes her fingers on her jeans, one hand at a time. She looks at him for a moment and sees him waiting. He can have a taste of his own medicine for a change.

'Personal question, Ahab. Put your seat belt on.'

11. Dinah

Within a week she found out that everyone at Kingsley High liked Queenie Collins. It would be hard not to. Dinah had never seen anything like Queenie, white hair that was wild and curly that on anyone else would look childish. But Queenie wore it like a crown.

She was good at everything, lessons, games, talking to teachers, carrying the right bag, wearing the right stuff and even if it was the wrong stuff not caring. Dinah did care. Dinah's mother said there was no uniform. She said 'wear whatever you like', so Dinah did, jogging bottoms and a T-shirt. Apart from Queenie all the other kids carried on ignoring her at first. They weren't horrible and they weren't friendly. They said hello and they said goodbye but Queenie began to include her at lunchtime and sit with her at the back of the class. She showed Dinah where the lockers were and the shortcut to the classrooms.

And Queenie was the only one who was a match for Lily and Layla.

Lily sat on the next table in the common room and pretended she was talking to Layla but it was really loud so everyone could hear.

'Is the new girl a refugee?' she said.

Layla looked over. 'She must be, or like an asylum seeker or something.'

Queenie was listening. 'What if she is?'

'I'm just asking a question,' said Lily. 'I mean, she's black so she's not English, is she?'

Layla joined in as well. 'She's got this like amazing millennial phone for poor people to phone the Third World and places like that.'

Then Lily raised her eyebrows and scanned Dinah from head to toe. 'And they're like pretty retro jeans. Like stuff from a backward country or somewhere. Like a donated outfit.'

Both girls laughed and said it together. 'Clothes Bank.'

Later that day they said it again when they walked past her in the corridor. 'Hey, Clothes Bank, can I borrow your hoodie?'

And again in the canteen queue Layla was talking so loud that everyone else heard. 'I can't wait for Saturday. I'm getting one of those tartan shirts with short sleeves.'

'Lush,' said Lily. 'Where you getting it from?'

And Layla said it even louder. 'Clothes Bank!'

Everyone knew. Everyone heard. Everyone laughed. But when Queenie stepped out of her place in the queue and went up to Dinah, the whole canteen went quiet.

'Hey, Dinah, take it off,' she said.

'What?'

'Take it off. Your shirt. Take it off.'

Then right there in front of everyone, Queenie pulled her hoodie off showing everyone her pink and black lace bra. Somebody whistled but the whole school held its breath. Queenie winked and held the hoodie out for Dinah.

Dinah took her shirt off but she had a vest on underneath so no one saw her bra which wasn't like Queenie's at all. Queenie put the check shirt on and Dinah put on the hoodie. It was still warm from Queenie's body. It smelt of Queenie too.

Then Queenie put her hands on her hips and did an amazing catwalk up and down the dinner queue, spinning at the end and walking back to Dinah. Dinah knew she was staring. She had never seen anyone with so much confidence and courage. She didn't care what anyone else thought, she was just herself, real and true. Dinah wanted to hug her. Then just before the teachers came to take Queenie to the headmaster's office, everyone started cheering and stamping and Layla and Lily looked stupid. It was the best thing that had ever happened to Dinah.

12. Ishmael

The narrow lane curls right and left for mile after mile and The Pequod is hard to steer. It feels like the tractor at Tanners Farm that Dinah had to struggle to keep straight. She can hardly see fifty metres ahead. The tall hedges are overgrown, leaves and branches scratch at the windows and Ishmael has to concentrate hard, keep her eyes open and go slow. It's so hard to pay attention and hold the wheel at the same time and try to remember all the rules of driving and to keep The Pequod in the middle of the road. It's exhausting. Ahab is constantly looking at a big map he folds and unfolds, talking about the names of roads or numbers.

'We can take the fork at Little Beeston then the B671 at Stanton. Or we could go left at Millingham and carry straight over the wold to Brackley Market. Not sure which is best at this time of day. Or there's the B4766. Of course, that might be flooded at this time of the year. Nearly impassable last year if I remember right. We don't want to get—'

'All right!' says Ishmael. 'Can you just say all that to yourself, please? I don't know what you're talking about. I don't even know where we are!'

And then *smash!* Something hits the windscreen. Ishmael stamps on the brakes as hard as she can. The Pequod screeches to a halt, stopping diagonally across the road.

'Shit!' says Ahab with both hands on the dashboard. 'What the hell was that?'

'I don't know,' says Ishmael, panting hard. 'I think someone threw something.'

'Get out and have a look. Hurry up in case there's another car coming. Hurry.'

Ishmael gets out, slowly, in case there is someone waiting to attack the van. But there is no one in the lane, no one in the fields that she can see. If someone threw a rock, they've run away. She walks to the front of the van and looks down to see what it was. A big black bird lies in front of The Pequod, its midnight velvet wings outstretched. It's the same colour as the one in Ahab's kitchen. Ishmael crouches over it.

'Please, please don't be dead,' she whispers. She touches its body with the tips of her fingers and it flinches.

Ahab shouts from the window. 'What is it?'

'A bird!'

'Well, throw it over the hedge and let's get going.'

Ishmael picks it up with both hands. It's heavy but there is no blood. She can feel its heart beating against her palms. Its eyes are open too, yellow and beady, scared. She knows how it feels.

'Don't worry,' whispers Ishmael. She carefully opens the side door to the van. She tips the rubbish out of the cardboard box and places the bird inside. 'We have to take it to a vet,' she says.

'Vet? Don't be ridiculous. It's just stunned. Leave it on the side of the road.'

'No!' says Ishmael. 'No, I won't.' She stares at Ahab because she means it. She has to speak up. He is first to look away.

'Great,' says Ahab under his breath. 'All I bloody need.'

He folds his map out again and then folds it back up. 'Get in,' he shouts. 'I know where to take it. It's a good half an hour out of our way.'

13. Dinah

Nothing changed when Dinah became a teenager. She thought she might feel different, more grown up somehow, closer to Jonah. But the next day was just another day, chores in the morning, lessons with Caroline in the afternoon. Jonah came late looking miserable and sat in a far corner of the yurt. Dinah tried to catch his eye but he just looked down at his hands or turned his face from her. Caroline told them both a story about a boy in the Bible called Joseph who had a coat of many colours.

'So,' said Caroline, 'because you're both so brilliant and gorgeous and clever and good, I'm going to make you both a coat just like Joseph's. But there's a catch. You have to get the wool, and dye it and spin it yourselves.'

Jonah grumbled something under his breath.

'What is it, Jonah?' said Caroline.

'I said I'm a not a ten-year-old girl.'

His mother put her hand on his cheek. 'No,' she said. 'You're nearly a man. A man who can learn to weave and sew so that one day he can look after himself and his family. Men and women, boys and girls, we are all the same, Jonah, and we can learn from one another.'

She walked them over the fields to Tanners Farm to get some wool from their sheep. Jonah walked far behind, kicking stones or picking them up and throwing them away again. On the way back they stopped at the Golden Lake in the middle of the woods and Caroline gave them both some pencils and some paper and told them to draw a picture of the coat they wanted her to make. Dinah was great at drawing so she started straight away. She was tired of trying to talk to Jonah or find a way to get him to be normal with her. So she just sat on the ground and started to sketch out her coat with stripes of red and purple and big square sections in sky blue and yellow. It was crazy and weird, with squares and stars and circles all over the place, and just perfect.

She looked up to see where Caroline was so she could show her the design but Caroline was standing at the edge of the lake and even from where Dinah sat she could see that Caroline was crying. Dinah stood up to go over and see what was wrong but Jonah grabbed her by the arm.

'Leave her alone,' he said.

'Why?'

'I said just leave her.'

Then he marched off on his own and Dinah didn't see him for the rest of the day. Whatever was going on, no one was going to tell Dinah. As usual she was on the edge of things, left out and miserable.

14. Ishmael

A mile up a dirt track, they pass a tiny one-roomed chapel, old weatherboard, silvered and warped. There is a single window and a single door and above the door there is a carving of two hands in prayer. It's definitely not a vet's practice but Ishmael doesn't say anything.

They park The Pequod and walk on a little way, slowly because Ishmael has the bird in the box and Ahab is leaning heavily on her shoulder. It's almost impossible to walk steadily. They stop in front of an even smaller house. In the overgrown garden, stinging nettles and brambles grow along the path and Ishmael has to kick them aside to help Ahab to the front door. She can feel the bird quivering against the thin walls of the cardboard box.

'Ssssh, little thing,' she whispers.

Under a thatched roof, a sign carved from granite swings in the breeze. 'Jeroboam House'.

'Let's see if he's in,' says Ahab as he clouts the door with his fist.

The man that comes to the door isn't like anyone Ishmael has ever seen; he is ancient and bent over, his white hair stands up in little curls like cotton wool and his skin is pockmarked and lumpy like he had a terrible disease when he was younger, but his eyes are twinkly and kind. He throws his arms around Ahab and pulls him inside.

'Ahab! Oh, what a surprise! Come, come, friend,' he says. He helps Ahab into a chair and gestures to Ishmael to sit down. The house is only one room deep, downstairs and up. Chunks of wood crackle and burn in the grate and the whole room smells of bonfire. There is a little sofa and an armchair and in the corner a sink and a blackened iron range. Above the mantelpiece there's a painting of a wide blue sky with streaks of silver clouds, and a lake, a memory that sits somewhere just outside Ishmael's memory. She's seen that place before.

'Well, a lovely visit and an unexpected one, Ahab,' says the man. 'Let me hear all your news. It's been many years. Tell me, how is—'

'Gabriel, Gabriel.' Ahab holds his hand up. 'We've only come because we had an accident with a bird. Show him, Di— Ishmael.'

The old man takes the box carefully and looks inside. He makes a little sound when he sees the bird, a kind of gasp. 'Ah, a raven. Come, my lovely girl, come.'

He sits down and takes it out carefully, lets the box fall and looks at Ishmael. 'You found her?'

'No,' she answers. 'She flew into the window while I was driving. I didn't see her. I didn't have time to stop. I didn't mean it.'

'So,' says the old man, nodding. He brings the bird up close to his mouth and blows on its feathers. 'She needs a rest. Needs to come back to herself.'

Then he looks at Ishmael and nods again. 'You're going somewhere.'

Ishmael looks at Ahab. 'Ahab asked me to take him to look for a—'

'No. You. Where are you going?'

She has to think. In that moment she could tell the old man, she could tell him everything, all the things that are bubbling up inside her.

The old man continues. 'Somewhere important to you, yes?'

'Yes,' she says.

The bird makes a noise, not a caw or a whistle but like an answer to something the old man said. He turns the raven over and holds his hand on the bird's back. He turns it again and blows one more time. The old man looks up at Ishmael and smiles.

'She needs to feel the warmth of my hands, that's all. It's not magic.'

'Is her wing broken?'

'No,' says Gabriel. 'I don't think so.'

Ishmael feels the relief wash over her. The bird won't die. She won't lose her wing; she won't be an ornament on someone else's windowsill. She watches closely as the bird in the old man's hand begins to move, begins to edge its wings away from its body, little flutters and flurries of movement. Ishmael is scared she will start flying around the tiny room and not be able to get out. Just as she's about to speak, Gabriel stands suddenly. 'She has done her job. She wants to leave you now.'

He takes the bird to the door. 'Open it,' he says but before she can pull it wide the bird flies up into the rafters of the little cottage. Ishmael screams. She can almost feel the raven's panic. It bashes against the window trying to get out. It flaps and clatters again and again against the glass. Ishmael can tell it's confused, it can't see the glass, just the sky outside, and it feels trapped. Ahab is stuck in his chair unable to get up without her help and the old man is too small to reach the raven. Ishmael will have to do it.

The raven flutters from one corner of the room to the other, cawing and diving. Ishmael opens the door as wide as she can and starts waving the bird towards her.

'Come on, girl! This way. You can be free! Come on! Here, here!' Ishmael pulls off her hoodie and starts flapping and waving the material, making a breeze in the little room, and the bird starts to swoop down. It swoops towards the door and then flies back into the room, swoops again and again until suddenly it dives fast and low and screeches past Ishmael, through the door, up, up and away towards the sky.

'Yes!' shouts Ishmael. 'Go, go. You're free!'

The bird circles the cottage and then it's gone.

'Oh my!' cries the old man. 'She spoke to you and you spoke to her. Thrilling!'

'She was just trapped,' says Ishmael. 'She felt trapped.'

'Yes, yes,' says the old man. 'And you knew it. We didn't. But you did. She's done her job.'

'What do you mean,' says Ishmael, 'that she's done her job?'

Gabriel puts his hand on Ishmael's shoulder. 'The raven is a spirit animal, a guide. When she comes she marks a moment, an important moment, and you must listen.'

He leads Ishmael inside. 'I don't know where you're going but she does. The raven means rebirth. And she means release. A new beginning. Does that mean anything to you?'

Ishmael nods.

'It was no accident,' he says. 'She wanted to find you.' The old man leans his head to the side. 'So, now I see it. You are Tego's daughter.'

Ishmael frowns. 'Yes.'

'You have the eyes of your father, my lovely. And something of his way.'

At the mention of Tego's name she sees Ahab wince, sees him struggle with his memories, but the old man goes on. 'Come.'

He leads them both to a side door and out across a small courtyard to the little church. He pushes the door open.

Inside is cool and clean and wide open to the rafters. The light through the little stained-glass window is blue and yellow and red, and patterns sparkle on the wooden benches. At the front of the church is a plain wooden table and a vase of green leaves and branches. It's the quietest place in the world.

Ahab grabs the edges of the pews and shuffles forward right to the front of the little church. He sits by the table and bows his head. Ishmael stands at the door with the old man.

'Tego was one of us,' the old man whispers. 'One of our brethren. He would come to our little church here sometimes to pray. He came for a few months before the Fellowship ended. He was troubled I think.'

Ishmael says nothing.

'The child will bring him happiness,' says the old man. 'A new child is a joyful thing. It's a girl, is it not?'

'Yes,' says Ishmael.

'A blessing,' he says, putting his small, wrinkled hands together.

'Not for Ahab,' she says. 'He doesn't know.'

'I see.'

'And it's not always a joyful thing and it's not always a blessing. Not for my mum. Not for everyone.'

'And for you? And for Jonah?'

Ahab turns at the sound of Jonah's name and starts hopping towards them.

'Sssshhh,' says Ishmael. 'He'll be angry.' The old man coughs and changes the subject.

'You must be hungry. Before you leave, let's eat.'

Back in the house, they sit by the fire.

'May I ask about Anne, your mother?' says the old man as he fills a kettle and puts it on to boil.

'Oh, Mum's fine,' says Ishmael. 'She's on a retreat.'

'And you didn't want to go?' he asks. He has his back to the room. He is cutting teacakes in half with a sharp knife and spearing them on long forks. He hands one each to Ahab and Ishmael. 'To the fire,' he says and goes back to his little kitchen.

Ahab holds the fork close up to the fire and nudges Ishmael. 'You've just eaten all those doughnuts,' he whispers.

'So?' she whispers back. 'I'm starving.'

Ahab grabs her fork and holds it next to his. 'You're too far away, won't toast anything the way you're going.'

Eventually Gabriel puts a tray down in front of them with tea, milk, sugar and a plate of little cakes. 'I didn't make them,' he says. 'I used to make bread and cakes for the gatherings. I was a very good baker in my time, was I not, Ahab? But my time has gone and all is made new.'

Gabriel sounds like he lived a hundred years ago. Like he swallowed an old book and he's coughing up the words. 'Tell me, Ahab, what of you? It's been a very long time since we saw you at our chapel. When you knocked at my door I thought you had come for prayers. It has been a long, long time, yes.'

'That prayer is my first in many years, Gabriel. I'm heading south,' says Ahab. 'And we haven't much time.' He hands a fork to Ishmael. The teacakes are toasted golden brown; jewels of raisins sizzle from the fire and as soon as she covers it in butter, it seeps into the crust and she can feel her stomach still aching for food. It tastes like heaven. She closes her eyes and the whole thing is gone in three bites. Both men are watching her when she opens them again.

'Ha!' says Gabriel. 'Man must not live on bread alone but Our Lord said nothing about teacakes!' He scurries back to the kitchen and pops another piece on the fork. 'Come you, to the fire with it.'

Ishmael has three pieces altogether and Ahab has four. Ishmael feels each teacake filling her up, making her feel a bit better inside. She feels some of the panic of the night and the morning beginning to subside. Gabriel watches her and smiles, his hands knitted together and resting on his lap, then turns to Ahab.

'So, Ahab, will you tell me what you prayed for? Do you want me to hear your confession?'

'I've nothing to confess,' Ahab says. 'And I'm praying for a van, a white van. I want it back. That's all. There's nothing to tell. A man came and stole something from me. Something precious and I'm getting it back off him. I have to. It doesn't mean anything to him and it means everything to me. It's mine.'

'I see,' says Gabriel. But his face is worried. 'And this van, why does it mean something to you?'

'His leg is inside it,' says Ishmael. 'He left his leg in it while he went for a rest.'

'It's not just that!' Ahab snaps. He stares into the fire and talks and talks, about the things he did, about each and every repair, every adjustment he made, about the hours and the days he worked on it, lived inside it, found the right bits, ordered them from America, from Germany, from all over the world because it had to be right. It was special.

'I have to get it back,' he says. 'I have to. I had a van just like it once. It changed my life.'

'How?' asks the old man.

Ahab stares into the fire and the light catches the tears in his eyes.

'Caroline. I thought I could make her happy. I worked on myself, worked on my temper. I tried. I really tried. Tried to be someone else. It wasn't enough.'

And Ishmael knows it's true. He wasn't always an angry man. She remembers somewhere deep inside, far back when she was a little girl, this same man squatting by the river with a frog on the palm of his hand. 'See,' he said to her. 'They're lovely. God's creatures.'

Now, she watches Ahab, older by many years, a broken man stroking his knee and screwing his fist into the empty leg of his jeans. Ishmael knows what it is to want something you can't have. He looks tired even though it's Ishmael that's done all the driving. Maybe he should stay here with the old man, maybe Ishmael should leave him and go on her way, continue her journey without him. She's just about to make the suggestion when she catches the eye of the old man. He looks at her and shakes his head like he knows what she is thinking.

'It's a shame about the weather, is it not, Ahab?' he says. 'This isn't good for the farmers. There will be floods again and land will be lost.'

'We could all drown as far as I'm concerned,' says Ahab. He beckons Ishmael to help him to stand. 'Me, you and the whole world. You can't trust anything any more. I used to trust the summer, the season when you wait for good things to happen, for the sun to shine on your skin, for the crops to grow, for everything to turn out well. The only season you can trust is the winter. Everything dies. You can rely on that.'

Ishmael feels the sadness oozing out of him and she wants to tell him he's wrong but right now, after everything she's done, maybe he's right. Ishmael couldn't wait to go to school, she thought it would change everything, that her life wouldn't be so boring, that she would make friends and find her place in the world. But it didn't turn out that way. You can't trust your hopes and dreams, you can't trust anything. Sometimes the best thing is to run from your dreams, as far away as you can.

At the door, Gabriel kisses Ishmael on the cheek. 'When you see your father, tell him you visited with me. Tell him I saw his face in yours. And kiss your mother for me. But remember the raven and how she found you. A new beginning is what the raven means, a rebirth. Remember that and go safe.'

Then he holds Ahab by the arm. 'And you, my friend, go well. And if you can't find peace, then make peace. Find the right path.'

Ahab doesn't answer, he just raises his hand to wave and then grabs Ishmael by the shoulder. When they are back in the van, he sighs and throws his head back.

'Christ! That was a bloody mistake.'

'Why?'

'Because no one will ever understand. Because prayers don't work. Let's get going. We've got miles to go yet. First we have to find somewhere to safe to park up for the night.'

15. Dinah

On the last day before the school broke up for half-term, Queenie invited Dinah to her house. 'We're going to Cornwall tomorrow but come over and we can just hang out.'

Hanging out with Queenie is everything Dinah hoped it would be. Queenie's bedroom is painted purple with silver stars on the ceiling and when you close the curtains they glow in the dark. She has her own television and her own laptop, she has the tiniest little speaker with a massive bass sound that she connected to her phone so that when they are listening to music it fills the whole room. Off the bedroom is Queenie's very own private bathroom with purple towels and loads of stuff for the bath, creams and lotions and make-up. And Queenie has her own mini-fridge in her bedroom with juice and Coke in it. There were no words for it. It was the best room Dinah had ever been in.

They are both sitting on the bed watching videos on the laptop. She can feel Queenie looking at her. She can smell Queenie's perfume and the chewing gum in her mouth.

'Why didn't you go to school, Dinah?'

It's not the nasty way that all the other children ask. Queenie really wants to know.

'My mum and dad lived on a commune and we all had lessons together. It was good.'

'Loads of you?'

'Well, me and Jonah. The other kids were too small.'

'Is he your boyfriend?'

Dinah feels a roll in her stomach whenever she thinks of Jonah being her boyfriend. She saw him in his bedroom at his new house with Caroline and Tego sitting across from her and talking about his new life and saying words like 'intense' and 'extreme' and 'awesome', sounding like someone off the telly. She tried to join in and say something clever or trendy but she didn't have the conversation and she didn't have the experiences Jonah had. He was going to college and going out to clubs and pubs and making new friends. He hardly asked Dinah any questions and when he did, Dinah had nothing interesting to say so he just carried on. Dinah felt a million miles away from him but she wanted them to be just like they were. That was never going to happen.

'No, he's just a friend. Sort of like a brother.' Even as she says it, she knows it wasn't true but she doesn't want Queenie to think that she has a boyfriend. She wants Queenie to think that she's available, ready to love and be loved.

Queenie jumps off the bed suddenly. 'Come on!'

Dinah follows her into the bathroom.

'Now sit on that stool and I'm going to do your make-up.'

Dinah draws back. What if she looks stupid, worse than before?

'What?' says Queenie. 'You don't even need it with that face! And that hair. Just let me put a bit of mascara on you. I mean, you don't need foundation because you're brown and you haven't got a single spot! It's so not fair. Come on, just let me have a go. Honest, it will look great.'

So Dinah lets her. Queenie is up close, she can feel her breath and watch her as she concentrates. She bites down on her lip as she slicks on the eyeliner, the touch of her fingers light and soft.

'Why were you all on a commune?' asks Queenie as she brushes colour on to Dinah's cheeks. They are so close it's easy to tell secrets. Dinah tells her everything, all about her mum and dad meeting, about their new way of living, about the disaster that was the New Bedford Fellowship and how her father and Caroline fell in love and everything turned bad. She tells Queenie about her mother and the way they had to scrimp and scrape for money and about the man with the one leg that lived in the farmhouse, and all the time she's speaking Queenie listens and doesn't make fun.

Suddenly, Queenie stops. She stands back with her hands on her hips and her head on one side.

'I wish I had your eyes,' she says. 'I wish I was different like you.'

'You're perfect the way you are,' says Dinah. 'Honest.' And she means it. Queenie is perfect.

'Oh and listen, ignore Layla and Lily. All they do is gossip. No one likes them.'

Dinah shrugs. 'They don't bother me. I don't pay any attention to them. Can't even remember what they said.'

Queenie puts her arms around Dinah and hugs her tight. 'Wow,' she says. 'You're so strong. I really love that.'

Dinah hugs her back but the beat of her heart is so fast she can't speak. She can't say, 'I love you too.'

16. Ishmael

They get to the supermarket in the next village just as it's closing. They hurry inside and just have time to buy juice and bottled water although Ahab even manages to moan about that.

'Water? Water? What's wrong with going to a tap? Or a river? The world's gone mad.'

The car park is empty so Ishmael drives The Pequod to the far corner near the recycling bins.

'This will have to do,' Ahab says. 'It will be quiet here until the morning.'

It's dark outside and the wind moans. It buffets the side of the van and whistles through the half-open window.

Ishmael helps Ahab into the back of The Pequod and they sit at the little table. She's stiff and tired. She's been concentrating for hours, watching the traffic, listening to Ahab, thinking about all the things she has to do, the things she has to take care of now her mother is no longer in her life. She'll ring home after a week or so and tell her that she's all right and not to worry. She'll tell her it was time for her go out into the world on her own. She won't tell her about Queenie because she wouldn't understand. And anyway, she's so ashamed she doesn't even want to think about it. She puts her head against the window and closes her eyes. Now is not the time for tears.

'Pull the curtains,' Ahab says suddenly. Never 'Please would you,' or 'Thank you for driving all that way.'

She does as he says. Then he claps his hands and points to a cupboard under the seat. 'Immaculate this is. Immaculate. Look under there and get out the blankets.' Ishmael does as she's told. 'Everything where it should be. I had this all ready to rock and roll. We've got everything we need for a good night's sleep.'

Ishmael feels her body tense. As usual she hasn't thought things through. There is nowhere else in this van to lie down. Even if she slept in the driver's seat with her coat over her she would still be in the same room as a strange and angry man. She feels a lurch in her stomach. Another bad decision.

'No!' she says, backing away. 'I'm not sleeping in there. I'll just stay outside. I'll just find somewhere else. Just give me a blanket, I'll . . .'

'What?' says Ahab, frowning.

'I don't want to . . .'

'Want to what? Come on. Chop. Chop. Up. Up.' Ahab holds on to the little metal sink and pulls a lever in the roof of the van. The whole roof goes up, up high in the air like a tent. He fastens something into place and tells her to climb up.

'Stop talking nonsense,' he says. 'Use the chair, stand up and pull the mattress across.'

And there it is, a lovely double bed, high up, covering half of the van with a little ladder to climb. It's wider than Ishmael's bed at home and it's all for her. Thank God. She closes her eyes and breathes out, a long deep breath.

'Go on up,' he says. 'I'll throw you a blanket.'

She climbs in and pulls the blanket over her. It smells of the outdoors, as green and fresh as a forest. She takes her coat off and makes a pillow, she lets her boots drop to the floor, she struggles out of her thick jumper so all she has on is her jeans and T-shirt and in two minutes she's comfortable. She feels her body relax, feels the tension ebb away and she can think again.

Below her Ahab is huffing and puffing. She hears him rearranging things and swearing or praising his own workmanship and how well something was repaired or replaced. She hears him lock the door and eventually everything is quiet.

'My bloody, bloody knee,' whispers Ahab in the dark.

The rain is light now and comforting. Every so often a car goes past. Ishmael hears it in the distance, listens as it gets closer and closer and then it fades away, somebody going home or somebody like her trying to get away from it. If it wasn't for Queenie maybe she would have never found the courage to make a new start, to be a new person, but she's done it now. Maybe that's something to be grateful for.

17. Dinah

The last summer before everything went wrong at the Fellowship, there was a trip to the Peace Festival. The summer solstice, when the days were long and the summer seemed to last for ever, was a wonderful time at the Fellowship. Everyone spent their days outdoors or having picnics and games. The Peace Festival on the moors was a special outing that Dinah went to every year. Hundreds of tents and vans all camped around an enormous bonfire with stalls for food and clothes and music. Everyone was in the Flower Van: Jonah, Ahab and Caroline, Dinah and her mum and dad, with a massive picnic and blankets and cushions and even swimming stuff in case it stayed warm. But just as they started down the track there was a crunching sound in the engine and the van just stopped.

Ahab was driving so Dinah thought he'd just get out and fix it like he normally did. He could fix anything. People from miles around brought their cars and trucks and farm machinery to him and he would get all his tools out and take the vehicle to pieces. He would spend hours and hours making everything right and eventually whatever it was would start working again. But this time was different. He just sat where he was and shook his head.

'That's it, I think,' he said. 'She's had it.'

'Oh no,' said Caroline. 'I can't believe it.'

'I can't sew it together any more, love,' said Ahab. 'She's just too old.'

Dinah looked at Jonah. They had been talking about it for ages, just waiting for the van to conk out once and for all.

'Can we have it?' she said.

Ahab turned round in his seat. 'What?'

'Can we have the Flower Van? We could push it down to the Golden Lake and just have it for our own place, just me and Jonah?'

The van was Dinah's favourite place in the whole world. It smelt of leaves and oldness, of all the times the two families had had a picnic by the seaside and played cards until late at night then taken rickety drives down black lanes all the way home. It creaked and bounced and sometimes it stopped altogether. None of the seats matched and none of the windows closed properly. Once upon a time it had been cream or white or something but now it was covered in huge, bright flowers that the children painted on whenever they wanted. It was Caroline's van but she shared it with everyone. It was just like her, fun and loud and all different bits of lovely things all mixed up together.

Ahab looked at his wife. 'What do you think, love?'

Caroline took a deep breath and then clapped her hands. 'GOL-DEN LAKE!' she shouted. 'Gol-den Lake! Gol-den Lake!' and then they were all clapping and shouting 'Gol-den Lake'.

Tego and Ahab got out and pushed the van off through the woods while Anne steered and Caroline clapped with Dinah and Jonah.

'GOL-DEN LAKE! GOL-DEN LAKE!'

The van was running away through the trees now and getting faster.

'Slow down!' shouted Anne but when Dinah looked behind, the two men weren't pushing any more. The van was just sailing downhill on its own and the lake wasn't that far away.

'Anne!' shouted Caroline. 'The brakes!'

The lake was getting closer and closer. Dinah and Jonah were shrieking because if the van didn't stop soon it would plunge into the water, all yellow and orange from the autumn leaves. But then it swerved to the right, skidded on the undergrowth and bounced to a standstill just at the edge of the water.

Everyone was laughing and gasping for breath.

'Hoorah!' shouted Dinah.

'Wow!' shouted Jonah. 'We nearly crashed!'

The two men ran up to the van to make sure everyone was all right.

'That was a close thing,' said Ahab. 'I was worried there for a minute.'

Then everyone saw Caroline with her hands over her face. Ahab ran and pulled her out of the van. 'Caroline! What's wrong? You OK? Did you bang your head?'

'No, Ahab,' she said. 'It's just the end of something.'

Ahab put his arm around his wife and hugged her. Everyone was watching, listening, and when Caroline spoke, she spoke to them all.

'This van was what I first noticed about Ahab. It used to be all white. He drove it into our congregation one Sunday afternoon and I fell in love immediately. I fell in love with the van first.'

Ahab was smiling. He looked like a schoolboy, like he must have looked when Caroline met him. He looked like Jonah. Dinah saw him as a young man, saw Caroline and Ahab as they must have looked many years ago.

Caroline looked at Ahab with huge, sad eyes. 'It was a wreck and he restored it and I thought to myself, anyone that can make something so beautiful must be beautiful inside. We used to go travelling in that van. We spent our courting days in it. Just us two. It was a long time ago now.'

'I even renamed it "The Caroline",' said Ahab and kissed his wife on the cheek, but there was a moment, half a moment, and maybe no one else noticed, but Caroline blinked and Dinah saw something pass across her face. It wasn't love any more.

18. Ishmael

Inside The Pequod is warm and dry. If it wasn't for Ahab shuffling and moaning below on his bed, she would be fast asleep.

'Don't suppose you've got any painkillers, have you, Dinah?' he whispers.

'Ishmael.'

'Or anything that might knock me out, Dinah? A little bottle of whisky, Dinah?'

'No. And it's Ishmael.'

'You warm enough, Dinah?'

'Yes.'

'Brilliant concept the Westfalia van, Dinah.'

'Stop it.'

'Stop what, Dinah?' says Ahab.

'Stop saying my old name all the time. It's not funny.'

'What's the difference?'

'The difference is I've changed. I'm someone else.'

'Fair enough. As long as you know that strictly speaking it's impossible. OK, then, *Ishmael*. I was just telling you about this van. Originally the roof was made of—'

'Who was that man?'

'Gabriel, *Ishmael*?'

'Yes.'

'Lay preacher, *Ishmael*.'

'Say it properly, Ahab. Or I'm going to sleep right now.'

Ahab chuckles to himself. 'All right, I'll tell you. Might take my mind off my knee. When we had the original families at New Bedford he would come and lead the service sometimes. You saw that little chapel? That's his own little church, his own little religion. He used to be a Catholic priest or something. But he didn't agree with everything so he left. Formed his own congregation. Only a few people left now. He believed that in the Creed of Wholeness we're part good, part bad, part animal, part human, part man, part woman. Can't believe I bought into all that stuff.'

'The Creed of Wholeness.'

'Yes, and depending on where you are in your life, one of those or two of those will be trying to control you. Used to make sense once upon a time. Anyway, he was the person that told me about the farm being for sale. So I sold up, put the word out, got a few people together. Dived in.'

'Who?'

'Who what?'

'Who dived in? Who was first?'

'Me and Caroline and Jonah. My family. Then you and yours. The Starlings, Elijah and Martha, Fedallah, remember him?'

'The Indian man?'

'Yes, him and kids.'

'I remember Pippa. She was nice.'

'Pippa and George.'

'Who was next?'

'If you had some morphine I could probably tell you.'

'Pippa had long hair down to her waist.'

'Yours was better. What made you cut it off?'

Ishmael puts her hand under her hat and strokes her bald head. She thinks of the dead hair in her bag and wonders why she brought it with her. At least her mother won't find it when she comes back from her retreat. Her head feels tender and itchy. It feels like the rest of her, not right, raw and too sensitive. She strokes her scalp over and over. She might let it grow out to a centimetre but no more. New starts mean getting used to a new her.

'Not answering questions, eh? All right, all right. Where was I? Yes, the Fellowship. Right, well, we were all running from something. Trying to find a better place where we could be ourselves. Where we didn't have to pretend. You can't know what it is to pretend, Dinah, I mean Ishmael. It destroys you.'

But she does know what it is to pretend. She has had to keep her feelings about Queenie to herself for weeks and weeks. She's had to pretend they were just friends but she wanted more than that. Just before she goes to sleep, Ishmael thinks of everyone she's loved: Queenie, Jonah, different boys, the one from homeschool, the one that smiled at her up at Tanners Farm. Then she remembers the beautiful black raven.

'Fly away,' she whispers.

19. Dinah

So the van died down on the shores of the Golden Lake and Jonah and Dinah began to use it to meet. They'd send each other a note and meet down there with sweets or cards or books. It was like their own secret home. No one else bothered with it. The tyres had sunk into the soft earth and two of the windows had fallen out but it was still cosy and snug.

But after only a few weeks Jonah began to change. He stopped answering her notes. He stopped talking to her. Jonah had been miserable for ages. Then he had stopped her when she was going to ask Caroline what was the matter when she was crying. Then he had refused to go to the Golden Lake for Dinah's birthday, and every time she tried to talk to him he'd just been different, cold, unfriendly. Was she losing him?

So, if that's the way things were, Dinah decided to go to the Flower Van on her own. She would stay down there until it was dark and then everyone would wonder where she was and Jonah would be sent to look for her and he'd know where she was and then he'd have to come down to the Flower Van and find her. Then she could talk to him and find out what was wrong and he'd have to apologise for being so horrible and then they could be friends again.

Dinah walked through the woods the way she always did. The path was covered with damp leaves, spongy, soft and silent. It was just going dark and even though she knew the way, she wondered if it was safe. The lights from the Fellowship houses disappeared the further into the woods she got until it was difficult to see where she was going. She heard noises she'd never heard before, animals in the undergrowth, whistles in the wind. She felt her heart beating hard in her chest. She should have brought a torch or a candle but she didn't think. She'd always been with Jonah before and she wondered if she should turn back. What if she got lost? She took a few more steps forward and just faintly, a few hundred metres ahead, she could just make out a dim light. It must be the Flower Van and there was somebody already in it. It could only be Jonah.

She got closer and closer, her footsteps silent on the damp leaves, but then she heard something. Voices. Voices that she knew, that sounded sort of familiar but different, like they were arguing or something.

Dinah stopped by the trees and listened but she couldn't hear the words. She crept forward now until she was only a metre or so from the van. And then she recognised her father's voice.

'I don't care,' he said. 'It's too late.'

The other person was crying and her father was saying, 'Sssh, sssh,' all the time.

'I can't go on like this,' he said. 'We have to do something.'

Maybe it was Jonah inside there. Maybe that's why he had been so horrible. Something was wrong. If Tego and Jonah were arguing it must be very serious and Jonah never, ever, ever cried. So if he ever found out that Dinah had heard him crying then he would be ashamed and that would ruin their friendship for ever. So Dinah crept back the way she had come and went home to the cottage.

Her mum was waiting. 'Where have you been, Dinah? Have you seen your father?'

'No,' said Dinah. She felt bad about it for months afterwards. She wondered why she lied, why she didn't tell her mother what she had heard, that she knew where her father was. Maybe if she had spoken, everything would have been different.

Tego says what happened with Caroline was all his fault. Caroline says it was all her fault or sometimes she says it was no one's fault. It was something that just happened. Ahab says it was because the Fellowship idea was a mistake in the first place and Dinah's mother never talks about fault. She says that in the end, people make mistakes and God forgives them. One day, she says, she will be able to be like God, but not yet.

Bang! It's black outside. The middle of the night. Something has woken Ishmael. She wakes up with her heart beating fast. She dare not move. She hears it again. A stumble and a groan.

'Christ!' It's only Ahab. The air rushes out of her lungs.

'Are you all right?' she asks. She hears him barging around into things beneath her. 'What happened?'

He says nothing for a few minutes. Everything becomes still again and she hears him sigh.

'Sometimes,' he says, 'sometimes I forget. I get a pain in my leg, the one I lost. It's real I tell you, as real as the other one. I get a phantom pain and I reach down and there's nothing there and the shock is terrible. It's like a nightmare all over again. It's gone and nothing can bring it back.'

Dinah doesn't know what to say. She doesn't want to think about missing things that used to be there. Her mother, her home, Queenie.

'And sometimes I even stand up or try to. I think I'm the man I was, whole, able-bodied. And I fall and I keep falling and I'll always fall.'

She imagines him staring into the blackness. 'Are you all right now?' she asks.

'Go back to sleep,' he says. 'There's nothing you can do.'

20. Dinah

It was the day after Dinah had heard her father talking to someone in the Flower Van at Golden Lake. It was supposed to be the day when Dinah and the other kids went to Forest Camp, when they all spent the whole day and the whole night in the woods up by Tanners Field and had sausages and burgers. Dinah was hoping they would have a surprise birthday party for her because there had been a funny atmosphere all week and Dinah thought that maybe there was a secret people were keeping from her. They might have made her another birthday cake, with more presents and songs.

Dinah's mum wakes her up early and tells her to get dressed but when Dinah comes down to breakfast, her mum is sitting at the kitchen table crying. Again. This is the third day her mum has been crying for no reason. She tries to hide it but she's not quick enough and Dinah sees.

Dinah's dad isn't having breakfast again and he hasn't come home again. She hasn't seen him for nearly three days.

'What time are we going to Forest Camp?' says Dinah.

'We have to go to a gathering,' says Dinah's mum, putting her coat on. 'Bring your toast. Eat it on the way.'

It's cold outside and Dinah's mum doesn't even tell her to put a scarf on or gloves or anything. She walks slowly up the track with her coat open flapping behind her. She has her arms folded and her head down and she doesn't even wait like she usually does. What's going on?

At the farmhouse everyone else is there waiting outside. Everyone except Tego. The door is suddenly unbolted and Ahab stands aside so people can come into the sitting room for the gathering to start.

There's never been a gathering before breakfast and there's never been a gathering without her dad. And there's never been a gathering where everyone looks so unhappy.

There is no fire in the hearth and all the chairs have been rearranged in rows, not in the circle that they usually have. Everyone comes into the room but as they pass Ahab they all say something like, 'This isn't right,' or 'You don't have to do this, Ahab.'

But all he does is tell Anne and Dinah to sit on the front row next to Jonah. Then he says nothing. He just stands at the door and even after everyone is in the room, he stands there holding the handle as straight as a soldier.

Dinah looks at Jonah but he won't turn his head. 'What's going on?' she says.

Jonah has a look on his face that Dinah recognises. It's the same look he's had a few times before recently, the look that won't let her in.

Then very slowly, Caroline and Tego come in, hand in hand. Dinah's mum keeps her head down and Dinah sees her tears drip on to her skirt. Dinah slips her hand into her mother's and squeezes tight. 'It's all right, Mum,' she says.

But it's not all right. Dinah's father and Jonah's mother are standing at the front of the room where Ahab told them to stand and they look like they are going to get married. Dinah saw two people get married at the New Bedford Fellowship. It was Pippa and George and all the children gave them flowers at the end and people sang and everyone kissed everyone else. But this isn't the same. There's anger in this room and sorrow too.

Ahab slams the door after them and everything goes even quieter than it was before. He stands in front of Tego and Caroline but he speaks to the whole Fellowship.

'When you become one with a person, when you get married, you have a ceremony, don't you? Joining of hands and all that kind of stuff? Make promises? Pledge your faithfulness? Say stuff like "till death do us part" or whatever? Yeah? You do, don't you?'

He looks from person to person. No one answers him. He even looks at Dinah but she doesn't even understand the question. She wishes she had an answer, she wishes she could say something to make this stop, whatever it is.

'So,' he carries on, 'it makes sense that when you get separated from that person, when that person decides that they are sick to death of their promises, then it makes sense that—'

George stands up suddenly on the back row. 'This isn't what the Fellowship stands for, Ahab. This is humiliating.'

'For who? For you, George? You haven't done anything wrong. Far as I know.'

'For them,' says George. 'For Caroline and Tego. For Dinah and Jonah. For Anne. And for you if you could only see it.'

For the first time, Dinah realises the truth. It hits her like a train and explains everything.

'Hang on. What are the rules, George? We all signed up to the same rules. That if someone called a gathering, if there was a special reason, if that person had a problem, then everyone had to support them and come. Everyone had to respect that person's right to speak. Remember, George?'

'This is making a mockery of everything we stand for, Ahab, and you know it.'

Before Ahab can speak, George and Pippa stand up and walk to the front of the room. They shake hands with Tego.

They kiss Caroline. They try to shake hands with Ahab but he turns away.

'Just go,' he says. 'Let's get on with it. This is my right.'

No one else moves. Dinah squeezes her mum's hand and feels the whole room fill up with sadness.

Ahab takes a piece of paper out of his pocket and unfolds it. He takes a deep breath and then faces Tego and Caroline.

'Tego Umbeke, you have chosen to betray your wife and your child. Caroline Matthews, you have chosen to betray your husband and your child. You have both taken something that does not belong to you. You have taken the love and the trust of another person and abused it. You have betrayed the New Bedford Fellowship and you have . . .'

At the back of the room, Dinah hears chairs moving and John and Mary come from the back and walk out of the room.

Ahab continues. '. . . you have made the decision to . . .'

Next to Anne, someone else stands and walks to Tego. He puts his hand on his shoulder and says, 'Goodbye, my friend.' He does the same to Caroline and then shakes his head. 'This is not right, Ahab.'

Ahab starts talking again, louder than before. '. . . the decision to . . .'

One by one, everyone leaves and Ahab has no one to speak to but Tego and Caroline. No one left in the gathering except Anne and Jonah and Dinah. They are all alone.

'. . . the decision to break your vows. This Ceremony of Separation is to mark the end of two marriages. To formally acknowledge before The Spirit and before our God that we, Caroline and Ahab, are no longer one flesh but two and you, Tego and Anne . . .'

'Don't speak for me!' shouts Anne. 'How dare you speak for me!'

She takes Dinah by one hand and Jonah by the other. 'This is not for our children, Ahab. This is not for anyone.'

She marches Jonah and Dinah back down the track. Dinah can hardly keep up with her. She can't see Jonah's face. She can't see her mother's face but she knows she's crying. And she knows that the thing that just happened has changed her life for ever.

Anne pushes the door to the cottage and sits Dinah and Jonah at the kitchen table. She puts biscuits in front of them with apple juice and grapes. She puts some paper and pens on top of the biscuits and then she puts a jigsaw on top of the paper and then books and a board game. Everything is nearly toppling off on to the floor but she just keeps putting more things on until Dinah starts to cry. Then Anne starts to cry. Then Jonah covers his eyes with his hands.

The day is ugly and dark and Dinah will remember it for ever. Her childhood ended that day.

Anne goes out of the kitchen and quietly closes the door. But Dinah knows she's crying silently. She doesn't know whether to follow Anne and sit with her but what can she do? What can she say? How can this ever be put right?

Jonah wipes his sleeve across his face and takes the lid off the jigsaw. Dinah watches him but she won't join in. She takes a piece of paper and writes on it. She folds it in half and passes it across the table to Jonah. Two words.

'You knew.'

Jonah stares at the paper for a long time, writes on it and passes it back.

'No,' it says.

So Dinah takes the piece of paper and rips it in half. Then she rips it again and again and again until it is tiny pieces all over the jigsaw. She writes on another piece of paper, folds it in half and passes it to him.

'Liar,' it says.

Then Tego opens the back door. 'Can I come in?'

Anne comes into the kitchen. 'What do you want?'

Tego steps inside and puts his hand on Jonah's shoulder. 'Jonah,' he says, 'your mother is outside. Say goodbye to Anne and Dinah.'

'Bye,' says Jonah. He slips a piece of paper on to the table and walks outside.

'Dinah,' says Tego, squatting down by her chair, 'I need to say—'

'To say what?' shouts Anne. 'What can you possibly say?'

Her father's face is different, all his skin looks baggy and grey. His eyes are red and his voice is husky and quiet. But he has lied to her. He has lied to her mother. He has made the whole world turn upside down.

'Go away,' says Dinah. She gets off her chair and stands by her mother. 'I hate you.' He says nothing. 'And I hate Jonah. And I hate Caroline,' she adds.

'I'll come back and see you,' he says with his strange voice and his red eyes.

'Get out,' says Anne. 'Leave us alone.'

'I am sorry, Anne. I am very, very sorry. I just fell in love. Forgive me.'

He puts his hand on his wife's shoulder and then, just like Jonah, he is gone from Dinah's life. She knows she could run after him for one last kiss, one last hug, but she feels the sorrow in her mother and she feels the hatred she feels for what her father has done. She stays where she is.

Later on, when it's dark outside and Dinah is clearing the table with her mother, she finds the last note from Jonah. She unfolds it and then screws it up in her fist.

'Sorry,' it said but it's not enough. It will never be enough.

21. Ishmael

Somehow it's suddenly morning. Ishmael opens her eyes and sees that the whole tent roof of the van is covered with leaves. The sunlight floods in, pale green and golden, and best of all, the rain has stopped. It's too early for cars, too early for people. Too early for Ahab. Ishmael has the world to herself. She can go anywhere with nothing to interrupt her. She can fly to America and walk the streets of New England where the leaves pile up in drifts, red and orange and copper.

She can saunter down the streets of New York City, live a new technicolour life in a technicolour city where yellow cabs blare their horns, where everyone would think she was just a regular New Yorker, a brown girl in a city of brown girls. Wear red lipstick or black lipstick or yellow lipstick. Grow her hair and dye it blue, bleach it white. She could walk through Central Park, go to a nightclub. Buy new clothes, jeans with holes and rips, T-shirts with pictures and slogans, amazing designs that would make her look like she was somebody. Tattoo parlours. They must have tattoo parlours in New York. She could open the door and just stand there and tell them to write 'Queenie' on her arm. And a 'J' for Jonah and a 'T' and 'A' for her mum and dad, all intertwined with one another, inseparable even though that's not true any more.

Or, instead of flying to America, she could sail. Stand on the deck of a ship and feel the swell of the water miles deep beneath her, see dolphins, seals and whales, watch the land disappear. Then she realises that every fantasy involves Queenie by her side. And that can never happen. She shakes her head to throw the thoughts away. She has to get used to being on her own.

22. Dinah

After one break at school, not long after that first visit, Queenie told Dinah they were going to do something mad. They were going to skip school for the rest of the day.

'We might die,' said Queenie. 'We might freeze to death. But it will be worth it.'

This was typical of Queenie, doing things at the last minute, without any plan but so exciting. But if they skipped school they would definitely be found and get into trouble and if Dinah got into trouble then her mother might find out and then it would be the end of school for Dinah. And the end of her relationship with Queenie. Dinah shook her head. 'I haven't even got a coat,' she said. 'Let's go tomorrow.'

'No. Now. Today. It's perfect weather. We need the wind.'

'Where are we going?'

'It's like high up the side of a mountain, like a really, really hard climb. Come on. We're going now.'

'But . . .'

But nothing. Queenie marched off out of the school gates. 'Now!' she said and Dinah followed her, to the end of the road, and then another road, and then through some fields, and then up a big hill, which got steeper and steeper and steeper, until they came to a cliff.

Dinah was still out of breath from the nearly vertical climb up Gulliver's Tor.

'Feel that, Dinah!'

Queenie held her arms out and stood close to the edge, closer than was safe, the valley spread before her.

'Feel it!' she shouts and beckons Dinah towards her. Dinah takes a step and another. 'Come on!' shouts Queenie and raises her face to the sky. Dinah inches towards the stony outcrop that seems to hang in midair, that juts out over the green fields like a pier over a lake, over an ocean. Then they're side by side. Queenie is grinning wide, her eyes on fire, and then she nods. 'Here it comes!'

Suddenly, *whoosh!* Dinah catches it, the violent, searing wind that rushes up from the moors and cuffs Dinah under her chin, that seems to have fists and fingers, that boxes her about the face and chest, bullies her, shakes her, and it's all Dinah can do not to fall.

She holds on to Queenie and screams into the wind. 'What is it?'

'Elijah!'

'What?'

'Elijah's Curse!'

Queenie drags Dinah away from the edge and they fall on to the grass, snuggling up to each other for warmth.

'It's wild!' says Dinah, tucking her hair into her hoodie and pulling the sleeves over her fingers.

The wind is so fierce Queenie has to shout into Dinah's ears.

'They say that if you stand there long enough, Elijah's Curse will knock you into the valley. It only comes up at the beginning of November, to tell you that the winter's coming and you have to prepare. That's what they believed in the olden days.'

'I've never heard of it,' says Dinah, shaking her head.

'You know what else they say?'

'What?'

Queenie's eyes are wide and bright. She holds Dinah's hand. 'They say that if you stand up to him, if you stand up to Elijah's Curse, scream at him, right at the edge, then he'll grant you a wish.'

They stare at each other and without another word they get up and carefully walk forwards. At the edge of the cliff, the stones and the rocks turn to bare earth. There's nothing between them and the ground so far below that the farms and houses look like wooden toys. Dinah feels the wind gathering in the valley, hears it rushing towards them and then it's back.

They spread their arms wide and welcome it, screaming and bellowing and laughing and holding each other tight, and all the while Elijah's Curse roars around them, rips at their skin, cold as death and ice, and it wraps itself around them, stinging their eyes and burrowing between the gaps in their clothes, slicing at them like a knife again and again and again, but the girls hold fast and scream and scream until their throats ache and then suddenly, Elijah's Curse has gone. It drops away, dies like a wisp of steam, and the whole world is silent.

'Quick!' says Queenie. 'Make a wish!'

Dinah closes her eyes and feels Queenie's hand in hers, feels her breath on her cheek and the grip of her fingers, and she makes her wish and she wishes so hard that when she looks at Queenie again, she really believes that it might come true.

On the way down the hill, Queenie starts laughing. 'I prayed for that coat in She Magazine with the fur collar.'

'What?' says Dinah. 'A coat? You prayed for a coat.'

Queenie shrugs. 'I come up here all the time,' she says and starts counting on her fingers. 'I've prayed for world peace, a cure for cancer, for my mum and dad to win the lottery so they won't have to work so hard, for water in the desert, and I even prayed for Amber when she got into trouble with Mr Oakfield. She was really nice but he was a creep. Oh yes, and I've prayed for you.'

'Me?'

'Yes, you. I came up here when you first started school and prayed that you would start smiling. You were so . . .' She makes a face like an unhappy clown. 'So now I can pray for that bloody coat and not feel bad.'

Queenie skips down the track laughing. 'Come on!' she says. 'You can tell me what you prayed for when we get back.'

But Dinah can't because what she prayed for was Queenie.

23. Ishmael

Underneath on the sofa bed she hears Ahab shuffling about.

'Morning, Ishmael.' He sounds better, not like he was in the night.

She smiles. 'Morning, Ahab.'

'I'm bloody starving,' he says.

'Me too.'

The supermarket opens at seven. They buy eggs and bread and orange juice. Ahab picks up a packet of chocolate biscuits, waves them in her face.

'Proper,' he says as he drops them in the shopping basket.

He buys loads of painkillers. 'The strongest,' he says to the woman behind the chemist's counter. Ishmael buys bottles of water and fruit gums, a bag of apples and some warm croissants that Ahab has nearly eaten before they get to the till.

In The Pequod there is a mini-hob with plates and cutlery, a little kettle, cups, everything.

They make eggs and beans but they are both too hungry to talk so it's half an hour before Ishmael pushes her plate aside and downs the last of the juice.

'My dad used to make this special breakfast called Pirate's Porridge,' she says. 'It was just normal porridge but he'd wear a bandanna and an eye patch while he was stirring it. He's so funny.'

She says it without thinking. Ahab looks at his plate. He turns it around on the table and presses his finger into the crumbs.

'Where do they live?'

'Near Oxford,' she says. 'Avoncliff.

'I mean what's it like, is it a farm or . . .'

'A cottage with a big field at the back. It goes down to the river. It's nice.'

She hears him suck the air in through his teeth, the same sound he makes when his knee is hurting.

'Jonah. How is he?'

Ishmael wants to tell Ahab about the last time she had seen him. Christmas, only six months ago. She wants to tell him that Caroline and Jonah have made a new family with Tego, that even though they say she's included, she's not, that even though they say she can come and stay she has no bedroom of her own, the new baby got that. She's on the outside as usual.

118

If she really wanted to be cruel she could tell him all about that new baby. She could tell him she's seen the photo. She could tell him that the new baby looks somehow like Caroline but with brown skin and blue eyes. She wants to tell him that she imagines her father placing his hand over the baby's heart and speaking in his own language, telling the baby all the stories that he used to tell her, telling her that she is special. That she has a big heart. That her hair is her crowning glory, the same as her grandmother's, the same as all the Kosi women. She imagines her father looking at the new baby, the way he used to look at her.

But she cannot tell him. Even though Ahab is angry and grumpy and shouts all the time and swears and never says please or thank you, Ishmael just can't tell him that Caroline looks happier than she ever did when she was married to him. She doesn't want to tell him that Tego and Caroline hold hands all the time and smile all the time because then she would have to think about Tego as well, and how he was never that happy when he lived with Ishmael's mother, when he was her father and her father only. Not the baby's, not Jonah's.

Ahab is staring at her, waiting for her answer.

'Jonah's OK,' she says. 'He's at college. He plays football.'

Ahab curls his fingers into a fist. He says nothing. He opens the packet of painkillers and puts four in his mouth. Too many. He gulps them down with some water.

Outside the car park is filling up with shoppers and someone is feeding glass into the bottle bank. The crash and clatter is deafening. It's too warm and stuffy in the van and Ishmael is dying to slide the doors open and let the world come in.

Instead, she puts the plates into the sink and brushes the crumbs from the little table. She pulls down the bed and makes everything neat but eventually she has to speak to him.

'Shall we go?'

He slides the door open and carefully climbs out. 'I'm going to the toilet,' he says and hops away.

24. Dinah

For days after Tego left, Anne hardly left the house. She would make funny dinners for Dinah, things like jam sandwiches that were usually only for treats. She stopped cooking altogether and even though there were no horrible vegetables, no aubergines, no courgettes, no cabbage, there was no nice stuff either.

Or Anne would buy soup out of a tin which she always said was no good because it contained sugar and additives but she would give it to Dinah anyway with bread or crackers or whatever was in the house. Dinah could stay up till midnight if she wanted but there was no television so she read her books again. Those days were strange and terrible and Dinah kept waiting for something to happen, for things to change even if they could never go back to normal. Anne didn't want to play or read stories in a funny voice, she didn't want to take Dinah out into the fields or to Forest School or art classes.

When Dinah asked if her father was ever coming back Anne just shrugged. 'I have no idea, Dinah.'

There was nothing for Dinah to do. She tried to make things better by tidying her room and washing up without being told but the noise of the vacuum seemed extra loud, the dishes clattered together in the sink and nothing seemed right without her father and Jonah.

The other families left New Bedford one by one. It seemed like every day someone else would walk by the house with something they were leaving behind to ask Anne if she could use it. A kettle, a table, an old-fashioned weaving loom. Anne took everything because, as she said to Dinah, 'it comes with their love,' and it was true.

They told Anne about how Ahab had gone mad. How he was telling them all to get off his land, out of his cottages, take the yurts down and the tents and leave him alone. Dinah would look out of the window and see him striding into the barn to work on his cars or banging around the shed. She saw him one evening staggering around like he'd been drinking too much. He was howling like a wolf. He seemed to have gone mad.

Pippa and George called round with loads of food and gave Anne their new address.

'We tried to talk to him, Anne. He's lost all reason.'

'I know how he feels,' she said.

'No, really, he needs help. Anyway, we have to leave, we have no choice. We're going to stay with my sister. We'll send you our new address. You might need it. You should try to get away for a while, both of you.'

Then Fedallah and Kito were next. They knocked on the door and stayed for hours talking about how things could have been different and how Ahab had destroyed the Fellowship.

'He's rude and aggressive. We're frightened of him. He came to our cottage and told us we had to leave and then locked himself away, refuses to talk. How can we reason with him? It's impossible. We should always act with love and that ceremony was cruel, Anne. I don't know how you could bear it.'

Anne was quiet, getting up from time to time to make tea or sandwiches.

'Have you seen him, Anne? Ahab needs to understand what he's done.'

Then all of a sudden Anne shook her head quickly from side to side.

'Sorry, Fedallah, but have you any idea what you're saying? He's in pain. Ahab is in pain. I am in pain. I know how he feels. You don't. OK, so it was over the top and it was stupid and he's made a terrible mistake but is it his fault? No.'

'I didn't mean anything, it's just that—'

'I notice no one is speaking about the reason for the ceremony in the first place.'

They looked at Dinah as if she didn't know. As if she hadn't worked out weeks ago that her father didn't love her mother any more and instead he had decided to love Caroline. That's why they left, because they were making a new family that didn't include her. They didn't even ask Dinah to go with them. Only Jonah. He'd thrown their old life away. That's why her mum was crying all the time, that's why all her dinners were sandwiches. That's why she'd lost her best friend and her father and why her mother was only half a person these days.

Anne carried on, quieter now. 'His marriage is over. He's got a broken heart and until you have one of your own, I suggest you stop making judgements.'

Fedallah started to speak but Anne stood up, went to the front door and opened it.

'Thanks for coming,' she said. 'Dinah, say goodbye.'

Dinah went and stood by her mother, snuggled into her side, and the two of them watched their visitors leave. They stayed like that side by side for ages. Anne stroked Dinah's hair. 'You beautiful girl,' she said. 'You don't deserve this. I wish I could make it better, Dinah. But I can't. I can't fix this, no one can.'

'It's all right, Mum,' said Dinah and she had never told a bigger lie.

25. Ishmael

The road climbs gently into the hills and Ishmael is driving The Pequod like she was born to do it. Fields stretch out, right and left, acid yellow and vivid green. Trees and bushes mark out the landscape into squares and triangles; sheep and lambs feed on the slopes.

Ishmael notices the small white stone cottages that look just like hers and the big farmhouses with barns and outbuildings that look like Ahab's. She pulls off her beanie and throws it on the back seat. The breeze is soft and curls around her scalp like a warm hand. It tickles and she begins to laugh. She turns on the radio but there is only a man with a crackling voice talking about banks. She turns it off quickly because right now she doesn't need anything.

There's a silver mist on the top line of trees where the horizon should be and then the hills disappear and ahead are wide open plains, a sea of green with a long straight road cutting through it. She drives The Pequod on through the countryside as Ahab sleeps in the chair. She's become good at the whole driving thing. She's confident and unafraid when another car comes towards her. She just pulls over and waves it past.

Come to think of it, you could live in a campervan like this. You could just park it wherever you liked and keep going, on and on through the Tunnel, to France, to Spain, to Italy. There's a bed and a kitchen, you can use the toilets in the supermarkets or service stations, buy a gas bottle when you have to, and fill up with petrol and food at the same time. Two people could be happy in a campervan. Her and Queenie. And if you had a big tent in the back you could camp in a field in the summer, or park by the Golden Lake and stay all summer.

Stop! She mustn't keep doing that, going back and back to someone who doesn't want her. Thinking of a future with someone she can't have. She has to think of something else. Jonah maybe or . . .

Suddenly, as though he can read her mind, Ahab starts talking in his sleep. Just one name.

Caroline, Caroline.

26. Dinah

Finally, when everyone had left, Anne seemed to collapse. She didn't eat. She didn't sleep. Sometimes, she closed her eyes but that was because she was trying not to let Dinah see her tears. It didn't work.

It was Dinah who became the mother, the protector, who made her mum get in the bath and lie on the bed. Dinah sat on the mattress and stroked her mum's arm because she didn't know what else to do. Anne had to be all right. She was the only person that Dinah could rely on. If her mother went to pieces then who would look after her? Her father didn't want her. He just took Jonah and Caroline and left. All she had left was her mother.

Dinah made toast and brought it up to the bedroom, which usually was against the rules, but her mum didn't eat it anyway so it didn't matter. There were no lessons. There were no stories. There was no father to tell them.

When she was a little girl, Dinah and her father were walking past St Mark's Church when the bell began to ring. It rang for ages which usually meant there was a wedding. They stood by the church and they saw the bride come out of a big car. She was wearing a white dress and veil and carrying a bunch of yellow flowers.

'I'm going to get married like that,' said Dinah. 'I want to wear one of those dresses.'

'And you will have flowers in your beautiful hair. And I will be there, very happy to watch. But, Dinah, the dress is only one little bit of the marriage,' her father had said. 'See how happy she is? That's because she's marrying someone she loves. That's what's important, Dinah.'

Now her father had a new person to love and that person was more important than his old life and more important than Anne and more important than Dinah. And he would not be there to put flowers in her hair because he was too busy to care.

Then letters began to arrive from Tego. He said he was in France where he'd gone with Jonah and Caroline, but Dinah put them in the bin. He had never taken her to France. One postcard said, 'I'll be back soon. I love you, Papa x.' In the bin. Then he sent parcels and presents in the post: a bag, a book, a bracelet. In the bin. In the bin. In the bin.

Then he started to ring. It was always in the morning. If Dinah answered it and heard his voice she put the phone down without speaking. She always made sure she got to it first, so her mother didn't have to speak to him, but once she was too slow. Anne picked up the phone so Dinah rushed over to her, snatched the phone, and hung it up.

'What are you doing?' Anne said.

'Saving you from having to speak to him.'

'Him?'

For weeks and weeks Dinah had watched her mother change, watched her turn to skin and bone, heard her crying at night, saw the black rings around her eyes and the light inside her grow dim. Dinah had to protect her from him. It was her job.

'You mean your father?'

'He's not my father any more.'

'Of course he is.'

'I hate him,' Dinah said simply.

'Whatever else has happened, Dinah, he loves you.'

'No he doesn't. He loves Jonah and Caroline. He doesn't love us any more.'

Anne put her arms out and Dinah snuggled into her. It was the first time her mother had seemed like her old self. She kissed Dinah's hair and let out a deep breath that seemed to come from the deepest part of her.

'All right,' she said. 'Dinah, my love. Life goes on. And we are alive, aren't we? And we have each other, don't we? And we are good and the world is good.'

'Is it?' Dinah didn't think so. Her world had become one of sorrow and pain and being left out and not mattering to anyone.

'It is,' said her mother. 'One day, this will be in the past and we will be happy again. Trust me. It's the end of something but not the end of everything.' She kissed Dinah's hair again and squeezed her tight.

'And there is someone else who needs us.' She stood up and put her coat on. 'Come on, sweetheart,' said Anne. 'We're going to the farmhouse.'

They had hardly been out of the house for weeks. Dinah ran and put her shoes on and was waiting outside the front door in less than a minute. Thank goodness she could go for a walk with her mother like she used to, have a change of scenery, a change from all the greyness at home.

Anne went into the kitchen and opened the cupboards.

'Oh dear,' she said. 'Not much here but this will have to do till I can go shopping.' She put some bread, cheese and a tin of soup on a tray, some biscuits and some milk.

They walked up the track and knocked on the farmhouse door. Not a sound.

'Run round to the back, Dinah. See if the door is open.'

Dinah skirted the farmhouse walls, peeping in the windows as she went. The whole place seemed dead without the families. There were no children laughing, no babies crying. No one was working on the allotment, no clusters of

130

people sitting together discussing things or mending things or just walking around. No Ahab.

The back door was open. She ran inside to the cold kitchen, down the hallway and opened the front door to her mother. Anne put the tray on a bench and said, 'Wait here,' but Dinah didn't want to be on her own in the big house with no one around. It was cold and dark and smelt of old food and dead fires. She followed her mother into the sitting room, then into the back room where the big dining table was that they used for meetings and indoor celebrations and where the children had their lessons. No one. The house was spooky and dead. Then they both quietly and slowly walked upstairs.

'Ahab? Ahab? It's Anne. Ahab?'

Nothing.

In the first bedroom there was a big double bed with all the bedclothes in a heap. In the next room there was a single bed, Jonah's room with pictures of rockets and space ships and dinosaurs on the wall. And there was a drawing Jonah had done of himself and Dinah wondered if she'd ever see him again. She felt her stomach turn over. He was still half here, in this room, all his drawings and the smell of him and all the things he used to love. All the things he had left behind including her.

In the next bedroom there is another single bed with no mattress and no other furniture. The thin curtains are closed

131

but a hazy grey light seeps through them. There is no carpet and then suddenly, she sees him. *Ahab!* Lying on the floor under a dirty white quilt. He is very still. Dinah gasps and covers her mouth with her hand. *He's dead!*

Anne tiptoes towards him and crouches down. 'Ahab?' she whispers.

'Ahab?' Anne says again.

Suddenly, Dinah sees Ahab's leg move a tiny, tiny bit. Then he rolls over and opens his eyes. Dinah moves closer.

'Are you all right, Ahab?' says Anne.

He moves his head from side to side. 'No.'

Anne and Dinah help him to his feet. They guide him to the room with the double bed and make him lie down. Anne covers him over and puts a pillow under his head.

'When did you last eat?'

'I don't know.'

'Right,' says Anne. She turns to Dinah. 'Go downstairs and bring up the food. Hurry.'

Dinah runs down the stairs and then walks carefully back up with the tray. Dinah's mother balances it on her lap and tears the bread into pieces.

'Go and put the kettle on, Dinah. And be careful.'

Dinah does as she's told and quickly runs back upstairs because she's never seen anyone as sick as Ahab before. He has a big untidy beard and his hair looks flat and greasy, his skin is white and looks a bit see-through and his eyes look like they've sunken right to the back of his head. If he's not dead then he's definitely dying.

He's sitting up when Dinah comes back and he's got a piece of bread in his hand. Dinah's mum is chatting about the weather like everything is normal.

'Thought we'd have some good weather by now but you know what April can be like. We've got a leak in the back bedroom, by the way, you might want to come down and have a look at it for us. We can't do it ourselves. And there's piles of logs to be split. This time of the year you need to keep a fire going, Ahab, or these old houses harbour the cold. It gets into the bricks.'

She's talking and talking but Ahab doesn't seem to be listening.

Then they heard someone open the front door downstairs. 'Dad? Dad?'

27. Ishmael

Ishmael thinks of what her life would be if everything had stayed the same. If she and Jonah could have stayed together and lived together. What would have happened to them? Who would they be now? The last time she saw him, at Christmas, he was different, he was becoming a man.

He looked better than all the boys at her school, taller, eyes full of laughter as though he had something funny to say, like everything was a joke, everything was clever, like he could make you feel that anything was possible. That's who Jonah is. And now he's got a new life at college. New friends. No one makes fun of him or his clothes. No one calls him Clothes Bank and leaves him out all the time.

And on top of that, Jonah has her father and his mother and a new baby. Now in some horrible way, he's got the life she should have had. One day she'll tell him how he makes her feel, that she's the one that should be living there not him. One day she'll find her voice and it will come up from the deepest part of her, a loud roar, and she'll tell everyone what she thinks.

She's hot suddenly and she's gripping the steering wheel so hard her knuckles are white. Then she notices the plains are gone, the fields have disappeared and the road is getting wider, faster, busier. Buses overtake her blaring their horns. Ishmael slows down as much as she can but it doesn't get any easier, everyone's in such a rush, and the more Ishmael drives on the more certain she becomes that they're coming to a really big town. Without thinking, she pulls off the road down a little side road that goes nowhere. She stops in front of a fence of barbed wire and as soon as The Pequod stops, Ahab wakes up.

'You were talking in your sleep,' she says.

'Where are we?'

Ishmael lays her head on the steering wheel. All she's done for hours and hours is concentrate and watch the road and move over and slow down and speed up and not drive into any ditches, and all the curves and turns and dips and hills on the road have been exhausting.

She opens her door and steps out. The feel of the earth under her feet and the electricity in her muscles, the sense of moving and walking and stretching her limbs, feel so good she starts to run. Then she's sprinting, vaulting over a gate, stripping leaves off bushes as she dashes past, throwing the leaves in the air.

But then, suddenly, a pain slices across her leg, slices into her brain. She screams in agony and falls, tumbling over and over, downhill, rolling like logs bouncing off the rough grass, being thrown again and again against the ground. The air is knocked from her lungs and she can't shout but in her mind she's bellowing, 'Help! Help!'

She crashes into the side of a tree and finally lies still. She can't do anything except gasp, try and get some breath back, but it's no good, the pain is everywhere. Slowly she opens her eyes. All she can see are the green leaves against the sky, the sun sparkling through the tree like it's a beautiful summer day and she's sunbathing in the afternoon. But it's not beautiful, the agony in her leg is ugly and black. She pushes her arms into the ground and struggles to sit up. Then she sees it. A long coil of barbed wire ripping into her jeans, into her skin, gashing into her leg. There's blood everywhere. She rests against the tree. She's got to get up but first she's got to uncoil the barbed wire and get it off her leg. Every time she tries to move, to reach for it, it digs in deeper, sharper, and she cries out.

She looks up and sees how far she fell. The hill isn't that steep. If she can just hobble up to the top, she could probably crawl back to The Pequod. Or she could call for Ahab. But he'll never see her down in the ditch. And even if he could, he can't get down to help her when he's only got one leg.

She takes a deep breath. She bites down on her lip and reaches forward. She can just see one end of the wire sticking out of her leg. It doesn't look rusty but it's red with her blood. Who left barbed wire in a field? Everyone knows how dangerous that is but people don't care. Someone could have thrown it out of a van or maybe it was left over from a fence. But really, that doesn't matter. All that matters is getting it off her leg and getting back to safety.

Ishmael has to be brave. Braver than she's ever been because this is going to hurt. With two fingers she holds the very end of the barbed wire and peels it slowly back. Immediately, it digs into the flesh on her leg.

'Aaaaagggh!' She tries again. The same thing happens. She feels the tears start to form but no! Not now! She can't just cry like a baby when something bad happens. She's got to get used to looking after herself.

'Come on, Ishmael!' she says aloud. 'You have to do it.'

She forces the barbed wire off her jeans; it digs into the soft pad of her fingers, digs into her calf. She draws the air in through her teeth and carries on. She winds it backwards around her leg, fifteen centimetres free. She does it again, unspooling it centimetre by centimetre, every single bit soaked in blood. She uncoils and uncoils until she is free and then rests against the tree. She's exhausted from the pain and fear. But she mustn't pass out.

'Get up, Ishmael!' she says. 'Move!'

But that bit is even harder. Her jeans are ripped and shredded by her ankle and she can feel the blood leaking into her trainers. She manages to get to her feet, holding herself against the tree. She thinks about moving the barbed wire in case any animals trip over it but she can't. Even thinking about touching it again makes her feel sick. 'Sorry,' she whispers to no one.

She pushes against the tree and hobbles forward. It's no good, she has to get down on all fours, like a cat, and inch her way up the hill. It's hard going. There are stones and rocks and her hands are sore where the barbed wire caught her. It takes ages, bit by bit, but she gets to the top of the hill, grabbing handfuls of grass and weeds to pull herself forward.

'Dinah! Dinah!' She hears Ahab's voice faintly on the wind. 'Dinah!' She never thought she would be glad to hear him call her name, even her old name.

She tries to wave but she's hidden by the long grass. She crawls and crawls, calling, but her throat is hoarse and she knows he can't hear her.

'Ahab!' she shouts. 'Help!'

'Dinah! Where are you?'

'I'm here, over here!' She waves one arm in the air. 'Here!'

She's so exhausted. She lies face down and waits. She hears him eventually. Scuffling and gasping. He falls down next to her and grabs her arm.

'What the hell happened?'

'I fell,' she splutters, 'barbed wire. Fell.'

'You've got to get up,' he says. 'Your leg looks bad. Get up.'

'I can't.'

His voice changes suddenly. 'Get up, girl!'

She looks at him. His face is serious. Just like him to have no pity. He doesn't even ask if she can walk. She gets to her feet and he puts his arm out for help.

'I can't,' she says.

'Yes you can.'

She grabs him and pulls him up and somehow, together, he on one leg and she with blood and gashes on hers, they shuffle and hop and sway and stagger all the way back across the field to The Pequod.

They crawl inside and Ahab sits on the little couch in the back. 'I thought you'd bloody well left me! I thought I was on my own.'

Ishmael stares at him.

He points at her. 'Don't you go running off like that again.'

'Is that it?' Ishmael says. 'Is that all you have to say? Not going to ask me how I am?'

'I can see how you are,' he answers. 'Look, I'm sorry, all right? I really thought you'd left me.'

Ishmael shakes her head. 'The Great Ahab. Thinking of himself for a change.'

'The first-aid kit is under the bench.'

Ishmael gets it out but before she can open it, Ahab grabs it off her. He takes a pair of scissors to the bottom of her jeans and cuts it away to her knee. He takes out some antiseptic wipes and cleans the scratches. Ishmael moans.

'It's not that bad,' he says. 'Was it rusty, the barbed wire?'

'No,' she answers.

'Good. You won't die then.'

He cleans the wound and puts some ointment on it. Ishmael keeps the noise of her pain to herself. She won't give him the satisfaction of crying.

He bandages the bottom of her leg and then puts the first-aid kit away.

'That's why you shouldn't go running off,' he says. 'Anything could have happened to you.'

'Yeah? Don't pretend you care, Ahab. Anything could have happened while you were asleep but you weren't bothered then, were you? As long as you get to your precious van. As long as you get what you want, no one matters.'

She grabs the scissors off him and cuts the other leg of her jeans away so they're both the same length. It's not tidy or neat, it's not even a straight line. It's a mess. She's got one more pair of joggers in her bag and that's it.

She climbs into the driver's seat. The pain in her leg is smarting. She says nothing because Ahab has no heart and doesn't care. She starts the engine and he climbs into the passenger seat.

'You can't just tear off without telling me where you're going.'

'Or what?' she shouts.

Ahab stares at her.

'Well?' she says. 'Or what? What will you do?' His beard has become wild and has flecks of grey in it. He has dirt still on his face but his eyes are wild and bright. 'And I'm not Dinah so don't call me that again. And I'm the driver, not you. All you've been doing is snoring like a pig and calling for Caroline.'

He jerks back. Her words hit him like a harpoon.

'Caroline! Caroline! Caroline! All the time you're asleep, I'm sitting at the wheel. I'm driving! And I'm tired. I'm so tired. Stop giving me orders, all right! You're not my dad.'

She turns away from him. 'Well? Which way?'

'Where are we?' he says.

'The next town is Keighley, wherever that is,' she answers.

'All right.' He looks at the map and traces a line with his dirty finger. 'We don't want to go into that town. It will be too busy for you.'

'I know that. I bloody well know that, Ahab. That's why I stopped. You've taken too many tablets. I've been all on my own with no one to help me. You've been asleep for ages and I've been driving on really shitty busy roads and making all the decisions on my own about which route to take. That's why we're here in the middle of nowhere and why my leg is ripped to pieces.'

'That's nothing. You try living with the sort of pain I've got,' he says, pointing to his knee.

'Oh yeah, how could I forget about your leg? It's not like you ever talk about it.'

She turns the key. Nothing. She turns it again and when The Pequod doesn't start, she closes her eyes so he won't see that she's nearly crying. She feels his big hand on hers.

'Easy,' he says. 'Crying's easy.'

She moves her hand away and turns the key again. The Pequod's engine purrs into life.

'How would you know, Ahab?'

28. Dinah

'Dad? Dad?'

Jonah. Jonah was back. Ahab sat up in bed and gasped. 'My boy!' he said. Then he grabbed the blanket and threw it off. He tried to stand but he collapsed in a heap on the floor. Anne pulled him up and he struggled to his feet. He pushed her away when she tried to help him again.

'I can manage.'

He pulled his shirt to cover his chest and tried to make himself look tidy but Dinah saw how thin he was and how terrible he looked. His beard was straggly and his eyes seemed to have sunk into his head. The room smelt of bad breath and sweat. He looked like the old men that sat at the side of the road and begged.

'Here!' he shouted but his voice was weak. 'Up here!'

'Dad?'

'Jonah!'

Dinah and Anne followed Ahab down the stairs. He fell. He shoved Anne and Dinah away but he was coughing so hard he couldn't speak. They stood back and watched him get to his feet, clutching the banister but moving quickly. 'Coming!' he spluttered.

Then there he was. Jonah. Standing at the bottom of the stairs looking up. Just as had always been, a big smile on his face, his hair all over the place. Dinah wanted to run to him and tell him how much she missed him. To ask him to come home and make everything just like it was. *Come home, Jonah.*

'My boy, my boy Jonah,' said Ahab and reached forwards, but before he could touch him the front door opened and Tego walked in.

They all stopped dead still. Dinah felt her heart thud. He'd come back. Jonah and Dad, they'd come home and it would all be all right. They'd made a mistake leaving her and the Fellowship. She moved towards him but Ahab stood in the way.

Tego looked worried. 'Ahab? Are you all right? Anne? Dinah? I went to the house but there was no one there.' He looked from one to the other, to his wife, to his daughter, to Ahab and the terrible state he was in. 'Are you sick, Ahab?' he said.

Dinah had no idea that Ahab had the strength to do what he did. He launched himself off the bottom step and flung his whole body at Tego. Anne screamed.

Tego held his hands up to fend off the blows and Jonah tried to hold his father back. But Ahab was a madman, a savage, a beast. He was scratching and punching and grabbing Tego's locks, pulling his head down to the ground.

'I'll kill you! You bastard!'

Tego raised his arms to protect himself. 'Please, Ahab,' he said but Ahab was wild. Jonah and Anne tried to get between the two men but it was no good, Ahab held on, shouting and cursing. All Dinah could do was crouch in a corner as she watched the violence, the madness, the disaster in front of her. Her father, her mother, Jonah. It was like she was trapped inside a nightmare as cruel and ugly as anything she could imagine.

'Dad! Dad!' she cried and then Jonah did the same.

'Dad! No!'

Ahab stopped like he'd been shot. Jonah held him fast. 'Leave him alone, Dad! Stop it!' he shouted.

'Go, Tego!' shouted Anne. 'Just go! You shouldn't have come here.'

But Tego stood still. 'I'm sorry,' he said. 'I came to say sorry. Dinah? I want to speak to you. Dinah? Five minutes, please?

Tego held his arms open but just as Dinah was about to move, Ahab pushed Tego's chest.

'Your wife is speaking to you. She said get out. This is my house. And I say get out. No one wants you here.'

Tego looked at Dinah but she just shook her head. She dare not move. Dare not walk towards him in case Ahab started fighting again. And anyway, her father hadn't come back for her. He had come to collect Jonah, to take him away again. He had come to say sorry but he wasn't sorry enough. If he was really sorry he would stay. If he was really sorry he wouldn't have left her in the first place.

She saw the hurt in his eyes when she didn't move. She saw the way his arms dropped down, heavy, empty. Then he turned and left.

Ahab pulled away from Jonah. 'Right, Jonah, go upstairs to your room,' he said. 'We'll talk about this later.' But Jonah didn't move.

'Upstairs, Jonah,' said Ahab again but this time with a fierce voice, with a voice full of anger and hate.

'I'm living with Mum now,' Jonah said. 'I just came to see how you were.'

'And I said get upstairs! You're my son and you're staying here. Upstairs!'

Jonah shook his head. 'No, Dad. I don't want to, I want to go with—'

'With him?' Ahab pointed at the open door. 'You would rather go with him than stay here with your own father?'

Jonah said nothing. Ahab walked right up to Jonah, as close as he could possibly get, until their lips were centimetres apart.

'You come here and put your hands on me. You come here and protect that bastard from the bloody good hiding he deserves. You come to my house and refuse to do as you're told. He's already having a bad influence on you.'

'It's not like that, Dad. It's just . . .'

'I tell you this, Jonah. You either stay here with me or I'll never see you again as long as I live. I will never speak to you again.'

Jonah's face seemed to crumple. Ahab's face was the same. They faced each other in utter misery.

'Please, Dad.'

'Never,' he said.

'Ahab,' said Anne. 'Don't make him choose.'

But Jonah did. He opened the door and walked away.

Then silence.

All Dinah could hear was Ahab panting, his breath quick and heavy. He looked at Anne but she sank on to the bottom step of the staircase and pulled Dinah towards her.

'Oh, Dinah, love!' she said. 'Are you all right?'

Before Dinah could speak, Ahab grabbed the door and flew out of the farmhouse.

'I'll kill you, Tego!' he screamed.

Anne and Dinah ran after him but he was too quick. He opened the door of one of his vans and jumped in. He started the engine and the van roared off with the door still open, banging as it careered down the lane towards Tego and Jonah.

'Tego! Look out!' shouted Anne and she began running down the track.

Dinah screamed, 'Dad! Dad! Move!'

The van was weaving and swerving all over the place. Too fast. Too fast. It missed Jonah by centimetres.

Tego was running now, his arms pumping, hurtling down the track, darting quickly from side to side trying to avoid the front of the van.

Suddenly Tego flung himself into the bushes and the van couldn't follow. It carried on straight. Faster and faster downhill. It carried on and on and on until it smashed into the wall of the cottage. It hissed and crunched. It seemed to shudder as the door fell off and the van tipped over on its side and then, finally, it was still.

And Ahab was still inside.

29. Ishmael

The cuts on Ishmael's leg are beginning to throb. She's got scratches all over her hands as well where she pulled at the barbed wire. Her jeans look ridiculous, like she's tried to make them into hipster shorts and failed. She needs some of Ahab's painkillers. They never had tablets at home because Ishmael's mum always had some herbal medicine in the cabinet. It worked better, she said.

If Ishmael was at home, she'd be starting the supper or watching telly. The screen is so small she has to sit close up to it huddled together but it's a miracle they've got one at all, even if it's old and rubbish, so Ishmael doesn't complain.

She wonders what her mum will say when she comes back, wonders what she's doing on the retreat. She'll be sitting with the other women, meditating or teaching. Maybe she's having a meal, maybe she's having a good time, but Ishmael knows how much her mother wanted her there.

As they pass through the towns and villages, the lights are coming on in the houses and cottages. It's going dark.

Ahab pokes her shoulder. 'Ishmael.'

'What?'

'I told you we can't drive at night,' says Ahab. 'Too dangerous. We need to stop.'

'We're in the middle of nowhere.'

Ahab has the map spread out on his lap. 'We're coming to a reservoir. If we're lucky it won't have any gates and we can park up there. They might have toilets as well. You can wash the blood off your face.'

Ishmael quickly looks in the mirror. She's shocked to see blood smeared all over her cheeks and forehead. When did that happen? And there's grass and mud on her bald head. She looks like she's been fighting wild animals.

Ishmael steers down a quiet lane, 'Broomfield Lakes', and into a big car park. There is a sign for coaches and caravans to the left and a sign for cars to the right. Ishmael drives left and parks the van near the toilets and Visitors Centre. There are only a few other cars around.

The injured leg is killing her, and the one that didn't get so scratched is still sore and aching from the hours and hours she's been driving. Her shoulders are bruised from the fall down the hill and she has a terrible headache. Without saying a word she opens the door and goes to the public toilets. They smell of old urine and bleach. She can't bear the thought of trying to get clean in there.

It's a beautiful evening, a dark blue sky, nearly black, but through the clouds there is the hazy outline of a full moon and light pools on the surface of the water that laps against the bulrushes on the shore. Ishmael walks along the edge of the lake, hobbling along, stretching her arms, easing her neck from side to side and scratching the itchy stubble on her head. Her feet are hot and sticky; the blood must have dried in her trainers so she bends down and takes them off. Her feet seem to expand immediately. She tiptoes into the water.

So lovely, so cool. She turns around to see where Ahab is but he's still in the van. She wanders further around the lake, where there is a little wooden hut. She stands to one side and slowly peels off all her clothes, right down to her bra and pants and the bandage. She shivers, the wind is just cooling. She edges closer to the water, feels the cold silky lake on her skin. She stands still and listens to the sound of the birds and the engines in the distance, to the sound of the night and faint music coming from somebody's bedroom, and all the things inside her that keep crashing together.

She moves forward carefully, feels the lake getting deeper and deeper until the water is at her chest, then she pushes off and she's swimming out into the inky blackness. She feels free. She feels the water, like cold hands on her sore, hot head. She feels the water, like a cold caress on her sore and wounded leg. She feels the water, like her mother's arms around her, soft and sure. She feels the water and she knows she could swim and swim for ever and if this water was the sea, she would swim to the land of her father's father, she would swim to Benin where the Kosi women live, and she would tell them of her broken heart and they would tell her what to do.

But there's no one to ask and she has nowhere to go and she's let everyone down, her mother, Queenie and, most of all, herself. She made a mistake and maybe if she'd stayed she could have put it right but it's too late. By now everyone will now what she did.

The next morning in her bed on the top of The Pequod, Dinah wakes up stiff and sore. She slept heavily and she aches all over. She bundles up her old ripped jeans and carefully pulls on her joggers. They're creased but they're comfortable. She changes her T-shirt and carefully puts on some clean socks. Everything is tender from the outside in.

There's bread from the day before, a bit stale but they eat it together in silence. Ahab is talking about the route and the van but Dinah isn't listening any more. She's heard everything he has to say. She puts a new bandage on her leg and some ointment on the cuts on her fingers. She carefully puts a plaster over the deepest cuts then sits in the driver's seat.

When she looks in the mirror she's shocked at what she sees: dark rings under her eyes, scratches and bruises on her face, and most of all sorrow. She sighs and shakes her head. How did all of this happen?

'You're a bit miserable,' says Ahab.

Dinah looks at him and says nothing. She picks up her hat and settles it on her head. She pulls it low so she can just see out of it. If she had her way she would pull it right over her face so he couldn't look at her and make cruel comments. He has no idea how she feels.

She turns on the engine and starts the van. She pulls on to the road with Ahab muttering directions all the time. She's so tired of listening to him she zones out.

30. Dinah

Dinah remembers everyone racing down the track towards the crumpled van. Tego was first to get there. He immediately turned round and shouted at Jonah.

'Stay back! Go to the house and ring an ambulance. Quick! Run!'

Jonah stopped dead. Dinah pulled his jumper. She could tell by the look on her father's face that whatever had happened to Ahab was very bad.

'Come on,' she said. 'Hurry.'

Anne and Tego jumped in the back of the ambulance. 'We'll be back soon,' she shouted. 'Don't worry.' But Dinah could see worry all over her face and she knew that Ahab was really bad.

Jonah was in a daze. Dinah guided him down the lane to the cottage and tried to help. 'He'll be fine,' she said, 'he'll be looked after.'

But Jonah couldn't sit still. He kept walking around in circles. 'It's my fault, it's all my fault.'

Dinah couldn't help, he wasn't listening. 'I'll make some tea,' she said but neither of them drank anything, they just sat in silence until Tego and Anne came back, hours later.

Jonah couldn't wait for them to get through the door. 'What happened? Is he all right? What did the doctor say?'

Anne and Tego looked at each other. 'It's too early to say, Jonah,' said Tego. 'You better ring your mother. She'll be worried.'

'Let's go back to the hospital, I want to see him,' said Jonah, grabbing his coat, but Tego held his arm.

'No, we'll go home. Tell Caroline what's happened.'

At the sound of Caroline's name, Dinah saw her mother wince. 'You better go, Jonah,' she said.

Tego just stood there looking at Anne, looking at Dinah, looking like he wanted to say something but there were no words that could put this right, they all knew it. He closed the door behind him.

The house was quiet then. Anne sat at the table staring at nothing and Dinah went to her bedroom. That was it. Her childhood was over and somehow she knew it. She knew that it started with her father's lies and the affair, then came her parents' separation and the arguments and him leaving with Jonah, then Ahab in hospital with injuries so bad that they couldn't even be spoken about and now, once again, her father leaving her behind. Nothing would ever be the same.

It was Anne who went and collected Ahab from hospital and took him back home. Anne who made Ahab a bedroom downstairs and nursed him back to health. He refused to see Caroline. Refused to see Jonah.

'Jonah's made his choice,' was all he would say. 'He's chosen Tego instead of me. He has to live with his choice.'

Sometimes Dinah was sent up with meals and washing and she had to go into his sick room and collect the dishes and the clothes.

Ahab would always be lying down with his face to the wall. He never said thank you, he never said please. The nurse came to look after the dressing on the stump of knee. Once, Dinah was there and she saw the terrible wound where his leg used to be. The nurse was chatting to Ahab about physiotherapy and getting fitted for a prosthetic and he wouldn't answer, wouldn't even look at her. On the way out, she shook her head.

'Depression,' she said. 'Look out for that.'

So Anne took Ahab to his hospital appointments and to see the doctor but when he came back he would just lie on the sofa with his back to the room. Anne would send Dinah up with a magazine about cars and vans and ask her to chat to him but all he would say was, 'Your father has ruined my life.' Or, 'Keep him away from me.'

But there was no need to keep Tego away because he never came back. Ahab lost his leg and Dinah lost her father.

31. Ishmael

'Ishmael! I said slow down!' Ahab is sitting up straight in his seat and shouting. 'Too fast!'

Ishmael has been miles away, a thousand miles away. She's been down the lanes of her childhood remembering, she's been sitting by the Golden Lake, she's been standing in the winds of Elijah's Curse, she's been everywhere but she's not been concentrating and now the road is falling steeply, too steep, and it's curving to the left, downhill, downhill, downhill.

'Use the brake, use the brake!'

'I'm trying!' But when Ishmael puts her foot on the brake The Pequod moans and there is the smell of burning rubber.

'Ease off. Ease back on. Quickly. I mean slowly!'

But The Pequod seems to have a mind of its own. It's like a dog being let off the leash and it's getting faster not slower.

'I can't hold it,' she shouts.

'Use the bloody brakes! Keep right!'

The more he shouts the more Ishmael feels the power drain from her body. She's lost control. There's nothing she can do. Ahab reaches over. He grabs the steering wheel and tries to hold it but they're bouncing and weaving like a ship in a storm. He just about manages to keep them to the right but they're still going too fast. At the next turn there is a big warning sign. A red triangle with an exclamation point on it and 'SLOW DOWN' in huge letters. This hill is too dangerous to drive.

They're going to crash. And if they crash they might die and if Ishmael dies she will never see Queenie again and she'll never see her mum or her dad or Jonah or the new baby, and now the brakes don't work and Ahab is half out of his seat with both hands on the steering wheel and the only thing that Ishmael can do is close her eyes.

She's not a real driver. She shouldn't be doing this. She hasn't passed her test. This is what happens when you do something you shouldn't. It's all out of control. She's way out of her depth. She feels The Pequod veer to the left. She hears a long, low moan and the sound of skidding that seems to go on for ever. She feels the ground judder underneath her and then Ahab screams, 'Brake! Hard! Now!' and somehow her legs still work and she presses down with every bit of strength she has left.

Screech. The Pequod scrapes against a brick wall. *Crash!* The Pequod stops suddenly, jerking Ishmael hard. She is straining forward but the seat belt holds her back, cutting into her neck and shoulder and squeezing every scrap of breath from her lungs. Ahab is flung hard against the windscreen.

Then a hissing noise from the engine. Then quiet. Ishmael puts both hands over her face.

'I'm sorry, I'm sorry,' she says. 'I couldn't hold it.'

Ahab says nothing. He will be angry with her, even angrier than usual. He will blame her because The Pequod will be badly damaged and he will have to restore it all over again. And now it will take even longer to get where they're going.

'Sorry,' she says again but when she takes her hands away, she sees why Ahab hasn't answered her.

He can't.

32. Dinah

'See,' he said to her. 'They're lovely. God's creatures.'

Dinah was just a little girl then, sitting by the edge of the water at the Golden Lake. She'd been there for ages watching the frogs hop in and out of the reeds, their black-green skin almost silver in the light. They croaked and moaned like they were speaking to one another, like they were a family all talking at the same time. Suddenly, she became aware of someone behind her. It was Ahab.

'Thought I'd find you here,' he said. 'It's dinnertime. I've been sent to find you.'

He squatted down beside her. 'What can you see?'

'Look,' said Dinah, pointing at some movement in the bulrushes.

Ahab slowly put his hand in the water and when he brought it out, he had a frog on the palm of his hand.

'Oh, he's a good-looking old boy,' he said. 'Look at the markings on his back.'

Dinah peered close and the frog blew out his cheeks and throat and looked straight at her. 'Why are they hiding?' she asked.

'Well,' said Ahab softly, 'not everything in the world is nice, some people don't like frogs, for example. Some people only like, say, cats or birds. They think frogs are slimy and ugly. What do you think?'

'They are slimy but I still like them.'

The frog croaked. 'He's saying goodbye,' said Ahab. 'We need to put him back now. He's got a family back there in the shallows.'

'Why can't I keep him?' asked Dinah.

'Oh, lots of reasons. Because he needs water and damp to survive, because he's a frog and he wants to stay a frog. But mostly, it's because somewhere out there at the edge of the lake there's a frog who loves him who he loves back. And all he ever wants is to be with that frog for the rest of his life. And maybe he's got little frogs waiting for him. So if we keep him, he'll be unhappy. And he'll be missed.'

Dinah watched closely as Ahab let the frog hop off his palm.

Ahab stood up. 'We all belong somewhere, Dinah. And if we don't go home, we'll be missed as well. Come on.'

Dinah took his hand and they went home together, through the woods to the warm heart of the farmhouse. But that was just one spring day and that was a different Ahab and they were different people then and it was a long, long time ago.

33. Ishmael

Ishmael screams. She's killed him! She reaches over and shakes him. Please, please let him be alive.

Every prayer Ishmael has ever known comes flooding into her mind, spilling off her tongue.

'Please, God, please, Great Spirit, please, anyone, please, please let him be alive.'

She unbuckles her seat belt and immediately falls forward on to the steering wheel. Her head feels too heavy for her neck and she feels like she's just woken up, woozy, tired. She mustn't fall asleep. She tries to focus. She puts one hand on Ahab's shoulder.

'Ahab! Ahab!' She shakes him but he hardly moves. 'Wake up! Please!'

She's dizzy but she has to get out. Get help. She flings the door of The Pequod open and tries to run to the other side of the van but her leg is agony. She drags it behind her as she scuffles behind the back of the van to Ahab's side. She yanks at the door but it's stuck. She pulls it with every bit of energy she has.

'Come on!' It opens a few centimetres but it just won't let her in. She forces her hand inside, her foot inside, and as the door slowly opens, the corner scrapes against the bandage on her leg.

'Aaaagh!' Ishmael screams and pushes the door open wide.

Ahab is slumped over forward with his head on the dashboard. She can't see his face but she can see blood.

'Ahab!'

She hears it then, faint but a definite groan. He's alive! But he's hurt badly. She can't move him on her own. She has to get help. She staggers away from the van and stands in the middle of the road. It's so dangerous but so what? Two cars swerve past her and blare on the horn. She narrowly avoids another. 'Help!' she cries. 'Emergency!' but they are going too fast to know or care.

Then she sees a red van. She stands right in front of it only a hundred metres away and waves her hands up and down.

'Stop! Stop!' she shouts. 'Help me!'

The red van slows and shudders to a standstill next to The Pequod. A big man gets out and runs over to Ishmael. He pulls her out of the traffic and holds her by her shoulders.

'Out of the way! Careful! You all right, love? You're bleeding.'

Ishmael can feel blood itching her neck. The seat belt must have scuffed her skin. Without waiting for her to speak, he dashes to the The Pequod and opens the passenger side door.

'We had a crash,' says Ishmael.

'Can see that, love,' says the man. He pulls his phone out of his pocket. 'Looks like you both need an ambulance.'

'No!' Ahab is suddenly alert. 'We're fine. We're all right. No ambulance.' He tries to sit up but almost falls out on the ground. The man grabs him and pulls him out but Ahab can't stand.

'You're all right, mate,' he says when he sees the missing leg. 'I've got you. Lean on me.' He holds Ahab under his arms and helps him to stay upright.

Ishmael pulls open the side door of The Pequod. 'In here. He can lie down.'

The man carries Ahab to the side of the van and sits him on the floor. 'What happened?' he says to Ishmael. 'I don't like the look of your dad. He really should have someone look at that head.'

The man has an enormous belly that hangs over his trousers. All the rest of him is thin. He has a shaved head like a big shiny dome and a thick gold chain around his neck. And a gold bracelet and a gold watch. He turns from Ahab and bellows over to his van.

'Get out here, Pip!'

The door to the red van opens and a kid gets out; he looks about Ishmael's age but so black-skinned he seems to shine. He has huge eyes and an Afro so big it wobbles when he shuffles over towards The Pequod.

'Make yourself useful, lad. Bring the first-aid kit, glove box. Quick.'

The boy shuffles away. 'Right,' says the man with the belly, peering closely at Ahab's face. 'Light wound. Not really bothered about the cut but the concussion's the problem. Did he lose consciousness? Did he pass out? Did you?'

Ishmael can't remember. She just remembers the skid and the brakes that didn't work. She knows it was her fault. She keeps hearing the screech, the sound of metal scraping and then the crash. She puts her hands over her eyes.

'Did you faint, love? Have you banged your head?'

'No. I don't think so. I think I'm all right.'

'Good. Right. Sit down there. Take your time.' He notices the scratches on her face. 'Looks like you've been in the wars already, love. Sit down.'

Ahab coughs himself into life. 'I didn't pass out. I know what I'm doing. Neither did she. We're all right.'

The man holds his hand out. 'Simon. I'm in Water Solutions. That's me. What's your name?'

Ahab opens one eye and nods. 'Ahab.'

'Right, now, Ahab, how many fingers am I holding out.'

'Seventeen.'

'Knock on the head makes everyone a comedian. All right. Where are you? What road is this?'

'Yellow Brick Road. Road to nowhere. Road to ruin.'

'We've got a poet. Thing is, mate, if you don't start talking sense to me, I'm going to ring an ambulance. Ambulance more than likely will call the police. And for whatever reason you don't want them here, do you?'

Ahab doesn't answer. Ishmael knows what Ahab's thinking. Driving without a licence. A young girl in charge of a van when she's had hardly any lessons. And a man that encouraged her to do it. Both of them breaking the law. If the police turn up he will get into serious trouble and so will she.

'I can answer the questions,' says Ishmael. 'We're on the A435 but I can't remember the town and you've got ten fingers.'

'Eight, as it happens, bab. Two thumbs. And it's not you I'm worried about.'

He squats down so that he's really close to Ahab's face and whispers. 'I did two tours, mate. Afghanistan, Iraq. Got one kidney and a scar down my back that looks like the map of hell. Know what I mean? Saw a lot of guys like you, injured, bits missing. Where were you stationed?'

'I don't want to talk about it,' says Ahab.

'Fair enough. Now, are we playing ball? Or am I going to ring 999?'

'Ahab, my name's Ahab. We're on our way south. We're going to a twenty-first birthday party. Friend of mine. I don't know this road, not been this way before. But we're on the outskirts of Birmingham, maybe north of Worcester. And you were holding up three fingers. Dirty fingernails. Wedding ring.'

'Fair enough.'

Pip comes back with the first-aid kit. Ishmael notices he's wearing one of the T-shirts she likes that all the kids wear at school, black with white writing on. The sort of T-shirt that Ishmael would love to own. The kind of T-shirt Queenie or the cool girls would wear at school.

Pip's T-shirt says:

```
BE COOL.
BE NICE.
SQUARED.
```

Simon starts taking out wipes and ointment and making Ahab sit still while he looks after him. He looks at Ishmael and nods to his van.

'Go with Pip, bab. He'll give you a drink of water. Got some chocolate in the cab as well. Get some of that down you for the shock.'

Ishmael follows Pip. Her leg is feeling better the more she moves it. She hopes she's not limping. The cab of Simon's van is covered with newspapers and sweet wrappers. On the dashboard is an enormous block of chocolate half eaten. Pip passes it to Ishmael who breaks a bit off.

'He eats two of them a day sometimes,' says Pip. They both turn to look at the man with his belly hanging low. He hands her a bottle of water and Ishmael gulps it down.

'What happened to your dad's leg or don't you want to talk about it either?'

'He's not my dad.'

'Were you driving? What happened?'

'The brakes don't work.'

'Spooky.'

'Spooky?'

'Yeah. We've got a song called "The Brakes Don't Work".'

'You're in a band?'

'Yes. Tangerine.'

'What do you do?'

'I write the songs and I play guitar.' He makes a strumming motion with his hands. He has long, graceful fingers and lots of rings. One nail has black sparkling varnish on it. He has lots of bracelets and bangles that clank together when he moves his arms.

'Is it OK if I have a bit more of this?' she says, breaking off another couple of squares of chocolate. It's sweet and soothing.

'Take the whole bar. It will stop Sumo having a heart attack.'

Ishmael laughs. 'You call him Sumo?'

'He calls me Pip, you know because of Tangerine. So I call him Sumo because of his belly. He's all right, really. I'm just a trainee. What happened to your hair? You've only just shaved it because your scalp's paler than your skin. That always happens. It will be all right in a couple of weeks. Your skin will go darker and it will match up. It was the same for me.'

He moves in close, roving his eyes all over her scalp.

'You've cut yourself quite a bit.' He touches her head and she flinches. 'Sorry, I didn't mean to, like . . . I should have asked before I touched you. My bad.'

His words sting. Ishmael knows he's right. 'It's not that,' she says, 'it's just really sensitive at the moment.'

'Suits you though. You look good with it. I didn't. I looked like an alien. My head's a funny shape under all this.' He waves his head from side to side and the Afro bounces up and down. 'Needs cutting down like a hedge.'

'I like it,' says Ishmael.

'Might keep it then,' he says and he smiles at her for a long time without saying anything. Ishmael feels a tug in her stomach, a rolling feeling like a fairground ride that makes her want to laugh. She knows she's blushing but she can't stop it.

'Do you live round here?' she asks.

'Nah, we were on a job. The first one I've done. Fitting a bathroom.' He holds his hands up and makes air quotes. "Water Solutions". Water solutions? It's just pipes and plumbing. Why can't he just say plumbing? I can't stand it.'

Ishmael laughs again. Everything he says is funny and sad at the same time.

'So,' she says, 'if plumbing is Water Solutions, what would an electrician be? Energy Solutions?'

'Shocking Solutions. Get it? Electric shocks. Your go. Carpenter.'

'Wooden Solutions. Tree Solutions. That was easy. What about a chef?'

'Belly Solutions or,' he nods towards Simon, 'in his case, Belly Questions. Like why. Like how.'

Ishmael laughs so much the graze on her neck starts to hurt. She puts her hand up to touch it, but Pip leans in and has a close look. She can feel his breath on her skin. 'Let me get some of that stuff from the first-aid kit.'

Ishmael stands against the red van and eats more chocolate. She's nearly had the whole lot with all of the water. She watches Pip walk away. He sort of shuffles with his hands in his pockets making his elbows jut out. His skin is darker than Ishmael's, much darker, and he's only about the same size as her but his hair makes him look really tall. The back of his jeans scrapes against the ground and it's all worn away and tatty.

Ishmael wonders how long it would take to make her jeans like that and where she would get the T-shirt from. Her jeans are ruined so she has to get some more anyway. She's got more than enough money to have a few new outfits now and Ahab will pay her as well so she could really get some great stuff. She could get her hair done in a hairdressers' when it grows out and she could probably get it into an Afro as well. And she'd still have money left over. Maybe she could get a guitar and guitar lessons with the rest and make a band with Queenie. Queenie and Pip.

How can they both make her feel this way, excited, nervous? How can she want to be with both of them? How can she be thinking about love when she's just nearly killed Ahab, nearly killed herself? Maybe that's what happens when something bad happens, it makes you think of all the things you want in your life, all the people that make you feel alive.

When Pip comes back he cleans the blood off her neck with antiseptic wipes and then puts some white cream on it. His touch is soft and delicate. He smells different too, not like the boys at school. He smells grown up.

173

'That's better,' he says as he presses a plaster against her skin. Then he turns her round and smears some more cream on her scalp. It tickles.

'Yeah,' he says, 'this is virgin skin. Not used to being touched.'

Ishmael can hardly look at him. His fingers are soft and tender. She never wants him to stop. She closes her eyes.

'What was your hair like? Are you, like, Asian or something?' he says.

'My dad is from Benin,' she answers.

'Where's that? I've never heard of it.'

'West Africa.'

'Right, OK, so you're half African.'

'Yes, but Africa's a continent. That's like saying you're half European. No one would say that, it's stupid.'

Pip nods his head. 'Yeah, I get it. I know what you're saying.' But he goes quiet and Ishmael feels sick for going over the top. Did she really call him stupid? Whenever she makes a friend she always says the wrong thing, does the wrong thing.

'I mean it's not stupid,' she says, 'I didn't mean that. It's just that because people don't really know about Africa, it's massive and people just think it's all one country or something. And it's my dad really, he goes on about it a lot so I always try and get it right. Well, he used to go on about it when I was younger.'

'It's cool.' He points at his T-shirt. ' "Be Cool. Be Nice." I practise what I preach,' and he gives her his long, slow smile that feels like being hypnotised. She can't look away.

'Where are you from?' she says eventually.

'Sri Lanka. I'm Tamil. From Colombo, well my parents are but I was born—'

'Pip! Pip!' It's Simon.

They both walk back to The Pequod.

'Give us your phone. Mine's dying. Second thoughts, you do it. Look up 24 Hour Vehicle Recovery. There's one on Red Lane. Find the number and tell them to get over here. Say Sumo wants a pick-up.'

Ishmael and Pip look at each other.

'What?' says Simon. 'Didn't think you were the first to choose that name, did you? You got to try harder, Pip.'

While they're waiting, Simon bandages Ahab's head, making him look like he's been in a real battle.

'We've got an hour to wait,' he says, 'and seeing as I'm in no hurry to get home, if you catch my drift, we'll wait with you. Pip has got to go to guitar rehearsal or whatever he calls it after work. Well, I call it work. Not sure what he calls it. He's good at the other thing though, so he tells me. What is it you do, Pip? Guitar or banjo or what?'

Pip doesn't answer.

'He's in a pop group, did he tell you? Called Grapefruit. Very sharp.'

Pip shakes his head. 'Pop group? Really? Anyway, we're starving, aren't we?' He nudges Ishmael. 'We're going to the garage. Want anything? Chocolate maybe? You look like you could use a top-up.'

'Funny,' says Simon. 'Just replace what you ate. And get us a sandwich each for me and him. Crisps. Orange juice or Coke, lots of sugar. Throw something healthy in. Apple or something. Here.' He gives Pip a twenty pound note. 'Buy something nice for your girlfriend as well.'

Ishmael feels her cheeks start to colour and she walks ahead so no one can see.

They strike out across a housing estate off the dual carriageway and come to the back of a small row of shops.

'Look,' says Pip. 'Fish and chips.'

'No way,' says Ishmael.

'Yes. Way.'

There is no queue. They are in and out of the chip shop in five minutes. The smell churns Ishmael's stomach and makes her mouth water. They sit on a brick wall and unwrap their packets.

'God, I'm starving,' says Ishmael.

Pip has a mouthful of chips and speaks out of one corner. 'Does it happen every time you get a bang on the head? It goes straight to your stomach?'

Ishmael smiles. 'I don't know, maybe I'm just so relieved but right now think I could eat fish and chips every day for the rest of my life.'

'Sumo', says Pip. 'Beware Sumo.'

Ishmael laughs. 'What's your favourite food?'

Pip says nothing straight away. That's because she's asked a stupid question again. Favourite food? Is that the best she can do? Her chips stick in her throat. Then suddenly Pip holds his hand up.

'Chicken! I had to think there for a moment but yes, I'd say any kind of chicken.' Then Pip squints and looks up. 'Chicken curry from Sri Lanka, like my mum makes. You can't beat it. Except maybe . . . actually, chicken and bacon in a massive baguette with mayonnaise and lettuce. With Coke and ice. Then cookie dough ice cream. More chicken. More bacon. Ice cream. And repeat. Your go.'

Ishmael thinks. 'OK. Johnny cakes. You won't know what they are . . .'

'Course I know!' says Pip. 'Fried dumplings. I love them.'

'No way!' says Ishmael. 'I've never met anyone who knew what they were before.'

'You'd never met me, that's why.'

And the smile again and the flutter in Ishmael's stomach.

'If you were staying around you could come to my gig tomorrow night. It's at the Old Fire Station in Moseley. It will be good.'

'Tomorrow night?'

The best invitation she's ever had and there is just no way she can go. She looks down at her hands. It's going to sound like she doesn't want to go. He'll think she doesn't like him.

'I wish I could. Really. But we've got to go to Dorset. Ahab had his van stolen.'

'Shame,' says Pip.

'Really, I mean, honestly I wish I could. I just can't.'

He looks at her for a long time and nods. 'I believe you. Maybe on the way back. Or maybe you could give me your number, just in case.'

He pulls his phone out and looks at her with a question in his big eyes but Ishmael doesn't know how to explain why she smashed her phone, or that it was rubbish to begin with. He waits for a while and then puts his phone away.

'Finished? We should get back.' He puts the rubbish in the bin and they go to the mini-supermarket to buy some stuff for Simon and Ahab.

They walk back slowly side by side through the housing estate. All Ishmael has to do is say, 'Can I have your phone number?' but the words won't come out and anyway, Pip might have already got the wrong message. All she has to do is speak but before she can say anything, Pip takes a pen out of his pocket and grabs her hand.

'Here you go. Free tattoo.' He writes his phone number. 'That's me. Don't wash.'

Ishmael smiles at him. 'I won't. Ever. I mean I will. I mean . . .'

'You'll find some paper and write it down?'

'Yes.'

'Good. Make sure you do.'

When they get back, Simon and Ahab are looking at the side of the van.

'You've got your work cut out on those panels, mate,' says Simon, gobbling down his sandwich. 'Could cost a bit.'

'I'm taking it to a garage I know. It's about thirty miles west of here. I'll be all right,' says Ahab. Ishmael sees how tired he looks and he's not eating anything.

'Where were you stationed, if you don't mind me asking?' says Simon again, quieter this time, like he's sharing a secret. 'Wasn't Belfast, was it? I had some good mates over there . . .'

'I wasn't stationed anywhere. It was an accident,' says Ahab, looking at Ishmael.

She saw something like sorrow in Ahab's eyes, like he was going to say sorry. It was an accident but it was Ahab's fault that Tego could never come back to the commune and it was a long, long time before Ishmael saw him again.

34. Dinah

Anne and Dinah went to meet Tego at a motorway service station. It was the end of summer and hundreds of people were milling around, halfway through their journey, taking a break, talking to each other, laughing, families going to see relatives or going on holiday. There was a little girl holding her mother's hand, two little boys with balloons, lots of children of Dinah's age milling around in a group or playing on the fruit machines. Everyone was excited or relieved to be out of their cars.

But Dinah sat with her father and mother and realised she wasn't part of a family any more, just the child of two people who had stopped loving one another.

Tego put his hand on Dinah's and said something in his language.

'We are the same,' he said. 'Big-hearted. And I have hurt yours. And I am sorry.'

Dinah moved her hand away. 'And Mum,' she said.

'Yes, and Anne. I am sorry.'

Anne had her hands in her pocket where he couldn't touch them but Dinah could see the effort she was making to pretend she was all right.

'So, Tego,' she said. 'What arrangements can we make for you to see Dinah, if that's what Dinah wants?'

'I can't come to the house, Anne. It's too dangerous.'

'He's not the man he was, Tego. You know that.'

'All the same, I've caused him enough . . . I mean, I don't want to upset him.'

The silence was ugly, all of them sitting there remembering the last time. Eventually, Tego leant towards Dinah and smiled.

'I would like you to visit me in my new home, Dinah. Would you like to . . .'

'Why?'

Tego bent close to Dinah and put his hand on her shoulder. 'Because you are my only child, my special girl and I love you.'

'Why don't you live with us then?' said Dinah. She knew the answer. She knew the answer made everything worse and ugly and that it was painful for her mother but she had to say it. She had to say it to hurt him like he had hurt her.

'Because your mother and I don't . . .'

Anne shook her head. 'Don't bring me into it, Tego. This is your decision. You didn't ask me before you made it.'

Tego looked down at the table and took a deep breath. 'I made a vow to your mother, Dinah, and I broke my promise. I said I would love only her and I now love someone else. And it was wrong of me not to tell your mother as soon as it happened. So I am sorry.'

Dinah suddenly smelt all the hot food in the motorway service station, the hot fat and the sticky sugar, and she felt like she was going to be sick. She put her hand on her stomach.

'Are you all right, Dinah?' asked her mother.

Dinah nodded.

'Let's just talk about the arrangements,' said Anne. 'Just stick to that, please.'

And then her parents talked. It was all polite and efficient and if anyone had walked past and looked at them they would have thought it was just a normal family that were having a normal conversation about decorating the bedroom or cutting the hedges in the front garden. They would have thought, 'Ah, lovely little girl sitting between her lovely parents.' But Dinah understood better than anyone else that you can never judge something from the outside. You have to be in someone else's head and heart, in someone else's skin to know what the truth is.

Anne and Tego talked about motorways and distances and dates and what Dinah would take with her and when.

'What's the address?' said Anne. She took a paper and pen out of her bag.

'It's a small cottage, a few hours from here.'

Dinah watched her mother scribble the address down. She wanted to tear it up and throw it away. She wanted to grab a piece of paper and write Jonah a note, to say she missed him, but she remembered his lies and the secrets he kept from her.

'Where's Jonah?' she asked.

'With his mother,' said Tego. 'You can see him whenever you want.'

'I don't want to see him,' she said. 'And I want to go home.'

35. Ishmael

It's almost dark when they pull up outside huge black doors that look like they lead to a factory or a warehouse. There are lights on inside and on the first floor there are curtains drawn and the sound of music.

'They're in,' says Ahab.

Ishmael helps him to the door and he knocks on it with the broom.

Someone in overalls with a big plastic visor over their face stands in the doorway. When the visor lifts, Ishmael can't believe it's a woman. She has a mess of red hair scrunched in a great lump on top of her head and a smile that breaks her face in half.

'The saints preserve us,' she says, looking Ahab up and down and staring at the bandage on his head. 'What happened?'

Ahab nods at Ishmael. 'Rachel, meet Di— Ishmael, meet Rachel, my sister.'

'Older,' says the woman. 'And wiser.'

'I need your help,' says Ahab.

'That's the only time I see you these days,' says Rachel. 'Come in.'

Ahab moves aside so she can see the recovery truck unloading The Pequod. It slides off the truck ramp and comes to a standstill, one side of it battered and scratched. The windscreen is cracked from edge to edge.

'Bloody hell,' says Rachel walking around it, knocking on metal, peering through the broken window. 'What happened? Where were you going?'

'Just patch it up,' says Ahab. 'Best you can do.'

'No, Ahab. No I won't just patch it up as best I can. Don't just come here after two years with your bloody orders.'

They stare at each other and then Rachel drops her visor on the floor and throws her arms around Ahab. It takes thirty seconds for him to raise his arm and hold her.

'Come on,' she says. She leads them through a garage, underneath cars that are up on stilts, past wires and trolleys, past cars that are rusty with no engine and too old to drive, past an office with an older leather sofa, car magazines on the floor, ancient posters about Health and Safety and one of a huge rainbow across a bright blue sky and, right at the back of the garage, through another door and up a flight of stairs.

The door opens to a warm and beautiful sitting room the size of the whole garage below. There are tapestries on the wall and leather beanbags instead of seats; the floor is battered naked wood covered with sheepskin rugs. Chinese lanterns hang from the ceiling, five or six of them, tasselled, square, round and oblong. And books. Books everywhere, piled up against the walls, piled up as legs for the coffee table, piled up as a stand for a lamp or a plant, more books than Ishmael has ever seen in her life. And at the far end of the room there is a kitchen and a long wooden table with metal chairs, more books and newspapers and a woman typing on a massive silver computer. She stands up when she sees Ahab and runs across the room.

'Well, well! You're alive!' she says and kisses him on both cheeks. 'And who have you brought with you to see us?'

'My driver. Ishmael.'

The woman holds Ishmael's hand with both of hers. She has the same brown skin as Ishmael herself, with a cluster of piercings in her nose, her eyebrows, her lips. She's as unusual as she is beautiful, with one side of her head shaved and the rest of her hair falling in locks, long black hanks of it, some matted, some smooth, some curly, like no one else, ever. 'Ishmael?' she says. 'Good name. How lovely to meet you. I'm Jude.'

Suddenly, she turns and pushes Ahab backwards and he falls off his crutch and lands on a beanbag. He gasps as she kicks the crutch away out of reach.

'Right,' she says. 'You won't get away so easily now, will you?'

Rachel and Jude laugh but Dinah sees the pain on Ahab's face and doesn't know what to do. Jude winks. 'Don't worry,' she says. 'He likes it. Go on, take a seat.'

There are four beanbags scattered around. Ishmael sinks into one and watches Rachel opening a little glass cabinet. She takes out four glasses and a bottle of whisky.

'A toast to the Prodigal Son,' she says. 'The Prodigal Brother.'

The whisky is peppery, hot and disgusting. Ishmael wishes she'd asked for tea or juice but it's too late now.

'Right, talk,' says Rachel. 'What happened?'

Ahab wipes his lips and curls the glass around in his hand. 'We had a run-in with a wall. Not serious but the van took a good bash. Road was slippery, oil on it or something.'

'You are the driver?' Jude says, looking at Ishmael.

'Yes. It was my fault, I—'

'Bullshit,' says Ahab, draining his whisky. 'Could have happened to anyone. The pads aren't great. I should have replaced them. And the steering column is . . . look, you'll see for yourself. Just get it as good as you can. Just so we can get on our way.'

Rachel shakes her head. 'Anything else, Ahab? You forgetting anything?'

'Like what?'

'Like, how are you, sister? Like, how's the business? Like, I've missed you.'

Ahab takes a deep breath. 'For God's sake, Rach.'

Rachel smiles. 'Good! Thanks for asking. So, let me tell you all our news.'

Rachel and Jude tell Ahab about the business, how they nearly went bankrupt, how they nearly had to sell everything, the garage, the flat, everything. How if it wasn't for Jude's graphic design work they would have gone under.

Rachel shakes her head. 'I actually seriously and really thought about going to ask Dad for a loan.'

Ahab throws his head back and laughs but it's not a funny laugh and no one joins in. 'Imagine the strings attached to that money, Rach.'

'That's why I didn't do it.' She looks at Jude, leans over and kisses her on the cheek. 'I was desperate but not that desperate.' And kisses her again on the lips.

Ishmael feels the whisky in her veins, feels it burn her throat as it goes down, and wonders what it must be like to kiss someone and then kiss them again and see their face light up, see them smile, not pull away.

Jude sees Ishmael watching her. 'Aren't you hot in that hat, my lovely?'

Ishmael slides it off her head and folds it in half.

Jude walks across the room and puts her hand over Ishmael's scalp. It feels strange, strong and familiar. She

188

turns Ishmael's head from left to right. 'Looks like you've cut yourself badly at the back. What did you use?'

'My mum's leg razor.'

'Yeah, don't do that again, sweetheart. See if you can get a buzzer, a proper one. And your leg? You're limping.'

'I fell over. Ahab bandaged it.'

Jude opens a cabinet in the kitchen and comes back with a tube of cream. She crouches in front of Ishmael and dabs it on the cuts on her head.

'Quick question, how do you know that miserable git there?'

'We're neighbours. I live at the farm cottage. The New Bedford commune, I mean it used to be a commune.'

'Well, he must have done some sweet talking to get you into driving here?'

'We're on our way to Dorset. He's paying me.'

'Well,' says Jude, standing up. 'You've got a long way to go. Stay here tonight. You can pull the van in so it's safe. Tell you what, I'll go and do it. He can't stand up and you look worn out, lovely.'

Jude puts on a coat and Ishmael hears her go down the stairs.

The whisky has all been drunk and Ishmael feels so tired she could fall asleep where she sits. Just curl her feet up on to the beanbag, close her eyes, stare at the lanterns and not wake up for days and days. She pulls her hat back on and snuggles down. Then she feels someone throwing a blanket on her and tucking a cushion under her head and then someone is taking her trainers off and someone else says 'Ssshhh' and then nothing. Just the sound of a door and an engine and footsteps and then a soft, sweet nothing.

36. Dinah

The first time Dinah went to the Sacred Women Retreat she was only ten. It seems a lifetime ago. Her mother went every year with the other women from New Bedford teaching the Sanctuary Workshop. Dinah would sometimes creep into the back of the tent and listen while her mother spoke about inner safety and the sanctity of the secret self.

Once she heard her mother talk about the Moon Goddess, that she ruled over all the other gods because without the moon there are no tides, without the moon there is no light, without the moon there are no seasons, without women there are no children, without women there is no life. Dinah was proud of her mother because everyone was listening but after a little while she was itching to leave the tent. Everyone looked so serious and quiet and Dinah felt that all the exciting things in life were happening elsewhere, certainly not in the Sanctuary Workshop. So she crept out again and ran off to find the other girls that she met once every year.

All the other girls under sixteen came from other Fellowships or other communes and they had their own special part of the retreat where they were taught healing and self-care, what would happen to their bodies as they got older, how to be sisters to one another, poems and stories about womanhood, and at night, the girls would sit together, singing and playing games. The retreat was great, the only time Dinah ever felt like she was at a proper party, and it lasted for seven days. All that time, Dinah would hardly see her mother. She would sleep in the same tent as all the other girls or in the wooden bunkhouse if it was too cold.

The parents and older women had their own tents and a sweat lodge and Silent Circle. According to Dinah's mother there were talks and long, long days of silence or reading or learning and everything that Dinah couldn't bear.

After Dinah's sixteenth birthday, Dinah's mother says it's time for her to join the adults.

'It's the Sacred Women in a few weeks' time, Dinah. And you'll be with me for the first time. You're a woman now.'

But Dinah is at school now and the Sacred Women's Retreat is in the May half term and she'll get behind on her coursework and her project and, most of all, she won't be able to see Queenie.

'I don't want to go,' she says. It's easier to talk to her mum when she's not actually looking at her, when they are doing something else completely, and right now Dinah is having her hair braided. All the knots and tangles have to be tugged out, then her hair is parted in two and oiled and plaited. It takes ages but at least it keeps it out of the way.

Her mother doesn't speak for a moment. She rubs oil into Dinah's hair until it shines. 'One day, Dinah, you'll celebrate being a woman. I know it's hard now with your body changing and everything but . . .'

'It's not that. I don't care about that stuff. I've got school work to do. I'll get behind.'

'We can do it together before we go.'

'I'm supposed to do it on my own. It's cheating if you help.'

Dinah's mother laughs. 'Oh, Dinah, it's not like that. Parents are supposed to help with their children's education. Mainstream school is full of contradictions, it really is. We have done well so far, haven't we? You're ahead in nearly every subject.'

Dinah jerks away from her mother's grip and turns round. 'I don't want to go!'

She bundles her hair on her head in a messy topknot, long tendrils falling over her face. 'You can go on your own.'

She runs upstairs to her room. One day she will be able to do whatever she wants. She kicks the door and it bangs shut. She stands at the window and looks out but there's only the same old view, the same trees, fields and nothing for miles and miles. Dinah drops on to her bed and looks around her room like she's seeing it for the first time. It's not Queenie's room and that's for sure. Her bed isn't covered in cushions and throws, the wallpaper from another century is peeling off all over the place and it's so small she can hardly move.

Her mother has had her life. But Dinah's is just starting. When her mum was young the world was different, black and white. Anne had adventures, she's always said that she lived her own life, that she spent years living all over the place, meeting people. Then for some reason she made the choice to go and live in the dead zone of the New Bedford Fellowship but that was only because she'd already done all the things she wanted to do. That's the point, she had choices.

What has Dinah ever done? Where has she ever been? There's a whole world beyond the lane and the crossroads and the pathetic village that doesn't even have a shop or a pub any more. There are kids in her class that are going to Italy in the half-term holiday. There are kids that have got holiday homes in Portugal and Spain, kids who are staying at each other's houses and going to parties and real festivals with no bloody Sacred Time and Silent Time and Prayer Yurts but live bands and pop stars, music and crowds of people camping and staying up all night.

Even the vile Lily and Layla are going to some wild festival at the beach and all the guys are staying in someone's house for the weekend. They were all talking about it. What was Dinah doing? Helping Mrs Tanner. As usual. Studying. As usual. Nothing. As usual. When everyone had been huddled in corners making plans for the holidays, Dinah had sat on her own and no one invited the weird girl anywhere.

Dinah unplaits her hair and tries to make the hairstyle she's seen in a magazine that one of the girls has at school. All she has to do is . . . first of all, she has to put it in a . . . No, that isn't right. It looks ridiculous. OK, start again. Tie it in a big scrunchie and wind it round on top. It looks even worse. And it's too hot in her bedroom.

She flings the window open and sticks her head out as far as she can. She feels the wind whip through her hair, the cool breeze on her hot scalp. The window overlooks the front of the house. She looks up the track towards Ahab's house and sees him walking to the farmhouse carrying a piece of wood, rocking from side to side because of his false leg. One man in that big house all on his own, only coming down to the house to tell Dinah's mother what to order or to collect his post. One man in a six-bedroomed farmhouse and Dinah and her mother squeezed on top of each other in a tiny farm cottage. It isn't fair. But then nothing feels fair these days.

She sits in front of her mirror and tries again. She wraps her hair in a big knot and sits it on top of her head and finally it looks all right. Not brilliant but better than she usually has it, hanging down her back making her look like a little girl. She'll be eighteen soon and legally that's an adult. Then she can start living her own life and the bloody Sacred Women Retreat won't be part of it.

Her mother opens the door and sits on the bed. 'I really wanted you to come, Dinah. But if you're ready to be a woman then I have to accept that you're ready to make some of your own decisions too.'

Dinah says nothing. It's as if her mother had been reading her mind.

'I have to respect your wishes, don't I?' she continues. 'Isn't that what womanhood is all about? Being able to control your own body, who you are and what you do?' She holds her hand out and Dinah sits next to her.

'So,' says her mother, 'why don't you go and see your father and your new sister?'

'I told you. I'm not going. I don't want to.'

'You'll have to sooner or later, Dinah.'

'No I don't.'

'OK, why don't you get one of your friends to come over and stay?'

'Here?'

Dinah thinks about the girls at school and the nice houses they live in with their big televisions and their laptop computers. She thinks about their bedrooms that probably have mini-fridges and nice bedclothes, that have posters of pop stars on the walls and music systems and everything that Dinah will never have in a scruffy cottage up a muddy lane.

'I'll just stay here on my own and do my work,' she says.

'I'll leave you some money for food and maybe you could make a pizza with that nice organic flour from the Mill. That'll be nice for you, won't it? And Ahab's up the road if you need anything in an emergency?'

'Emergency?'

'Well, he's always there and it's only up the track so you won't be on your own.'

'Yeah, great.'

Dinah's mother gets up off the bed and stands in the doorway. 'I'll go to the retreat. Maybe Sophie will come with me, eh? You know, the woman from the health food shop in Newcastle? She's always asking me about it. We could make a little holiday out of it.' She leans over and kisses Dinah on the top of her head. 'It won't be the same without you, though.'

There is pain in her mother's voice and if Dinah wasn't so mixed up and worried then she might have run after her and hugged her and said she'd changed her mind and the two of them would have made plans together, and she could pretend to get excited about what they would do at the Sacred Women Retreat and they would spend the night remembering all the other times they'd been. But it's too late.

Her mother is downstairs with a heavy heart, making a dinner neither of them wants to eat, and all Dinah can think about is tomorrow, back to school.

Back to Queenie.

37. Ishmael

It's bright sunshine in the sitting room when Dinah wakes up. She opens her eyes and closes them again. She has never felt so comfortable. She feels like she's slept for days instead of just one night.

For a moment she thinks she's at home in bed and then she remembers; she's with Ahab at his sister's house and his sister has a girlfriend. Or a wife. She hears them all in the kitchen.

Rachel's speaking. 'Five years is a long time, Ahab. Don't you think you've lost enough?'

'My leg, you mean?'

'I don't mean that and you know it. You've drowned yourself in engine oil, in sliding under vans and burying yourself away. You've lost your way.'

They have all gone quiet. Ishmael has to strain to hear Ahab.

'I thought about . . .'

'What?'

'You know, an online dating site.'

'Why not?'

'I spent ages writing a good profile. I wanted it to be truthful but, you know, give a sense of who I am deep inside.'

'Good idea.'

'Want to hear it?'

'Course I do.'

Ahab clears his throat. 'Ex-good-looking man, late forties, own teeth and hair, seeks faithful, emphasis on *faithful* woman, for fabulous lifestyle of luxury in plush old farmhouse located in remote ex-commune of misfits. Must have affinity with one-legged mechanics and possess strong shoulders for leaning on physically and figuratively. Avoid if you think you'll ever need protecting from say burglars or mad dogs as it's never going to happen. Apply now before I'm snapped up.'

No one says anything. She imagines Ahab kneading his knee and hanging his head or looking them both straight in the eye with his mouth turned down at the corners.

'Christ,' Rachel says. 'You're a miserable bastard. What does that boy see in you?'

'What boy?' says Ahab.

'Five guesses.'

'Do you still see him?'

'Of course I bloody well see him. Whenever I can. He's my nephew. Jonah's the most lovely kid, Ahab, and you're missing out on your son's life. If it was me and you'd ignored me for half of my life I wouldn't have anything to do with you but he's not like us. He's not hard. He asks about you all the time. Jonah's a really great kid and—'

Jude speaks over Rachel. 'And you, mate, need a kick up the arse and you always have. What are you waiting for? Come on, Ahab. I've known you nearly as long as she has and you've always been the same. You get fixated on things and take everything so personally.'

'So I suppose Caroline didn't personally leave me and personally take my child and then personally make a new life for him with a new father and . . .'

'She was angry and she was scared. Don't forget what you did back then as well. You frighten people with your bloody temper, Ahab. She's calmed down now. She was so young when you two got together. People change. She grew up and, listen, just make peace with the past, can't you? It would be a good time to go and make friends again, for Jonah's sake. It was a long time ago, Ahab, for God's sake. Remember when you and me split up. You knew I was gay before I did but you still nursed a grudge, didn't you?'

'That was years ago.'

Ever so slowly Ishmael turns over in bed and looks at Ahab. She wonders what he was like when he was young and how he knew she was gay and what he thought, and she thinks about asking him and telling him everything. Maybe underneath it all there's something good and wise. But no, he's still Ahab and he wouldn't understand.

Rachel laughs. 'Yes, exactly. Look, Caroline fell in love with someone else. It happens.'

'Easy for you to say.'

'No it isn't. Love isn't easy. Never. Look what Dad did to me when I fell in love with her.'

'It's not the same.'

'Isn't it? He cut me off without a word. Said I'd brought disgrace on the congregation, said I was Satan's child? How do you think that felt? I had to leave home, nobody spoke to me, lost both my parents in one day. You didn't. You were the golden boy in those days, faithful to the Lord and all that. Listen, Ahab, you make sacrifices for the things you love, and you love Jonah, I know you do. Go and see him.'

'I can't.'

'Why not? Because you made some big pronouncement? Because of your pride? Don't be such an idiot. Climb down off your high horse and go and see him.'

'And watch Caroline all loved up, all kissy, kissy with that bastard? I don't think so.'

Ishmael feels the hammer of her heart. She feels sick in her stomach. That bastard is her father. She throws the blanket off and stands up. They all turn around.

She puts her feet in her boots. 'I'm going out for some fresh air.'

Jude follows.

Outside, the morning is crisp and cold. Ishmael folds her coat tight around her chest and leans against the garage doors. Jude does the same, rolling a cigarette although she already has one in her mouth. Ishmael takes a deep breath and lets it out slowly. What she really wants to do is run off and leave Ahab to find his own bloody way south.

'That bad, eh, my lovely?' says Jude, not taking her eyes off her cigarette papers.

Ishmael nods. 'Is Rachel your girlfriend or your wife?'

'Both. Always.'

'How long . . . I mean, did you always know?'

'That I was gay? Yes but it was hard to accept in those days. Probably still is. Anyway, I had boyfriends for a while, trying to fit in, you know. Ahab was one of them. But through him I met Rachel and I just knew. I mean, I knew but she didn't.' She points at her heart. 'I knew in here that all I had to do was wait.'

'How long did you have to wait?'

'About seven years, I think.'

Ishmael closes her eyes. Seven years. That might as well be forever.

Jude lights her new cigarette. 'So, do you want to tell me who she is?'

'Someone at school.'

'But she doesn't know you're gay, right? Does anyone know? Does your mum? Your dad? Ahab?'

Ishmael would never be able to make anyone understand. It's too complicated and jumbled up inside of her. She doesn't have the words.

'What about boys?' says Jude. 'Do you like boys?'

'Sometimes.'

'And you're confused, right?'

Ishmael shrugs.

'You're mixed race like me, aren't you?'

'Yes.'

'Black and white, yeah?'

'Yes.'

'Neither? Both?'

'Sort of.'

'You should think about that. Neither. Both. Sort of. There's an answer in there somewhere.'

Jude smokes her second cigarette, blowing white smoke rings that float away and dissolve against the sky.

'Word of advice, Ishmael,' says Jude when she's finished. 'Always be yourself first.' She taps Ishmael's heart. 'In there, find yourself and be yourself. Please other people, yes, but be yourself first.'

Then Jude hugs Ishmael so hard she nearly squeezes the tears out. Jude kisses her on her forehead.

'Doesn't get easier, sweetheart. But it does get to be worth it.'

Ishmael smiles, a sad smile.

'Actually, I just lied. It does get easier. Find your tribe. Then it gets easier.'

38. Dinah

The day after Anne left for the women's retreat Dinah finds herself back in Queenie's bedroom. It was only three days ago. The two girls lie side by side.

Dinah isn't really watching the band on Queenie's phone. She isn't really listening to the music. She's thinking the same thing over and over. Is this the right time to say it?

'My dad will be in soon,' says Queenie. 'If he drives you home, you don't have to take the bus. You can stay for ages.'

'Great,' says Dinah. She notices that even though Queenie's hair is blonde her eyelashes are dark brown like her eyes. She's got lots of unusual things about her like that. And even though Dinah's skin is brown, Queenie is even darker because she's just come back from holiday. She went skiing in the Easter break and got a suntan. It sounds impossible to Dinah. To go somewhere cold and come back brown.

Everyone else was revising but somehow Queenie never seems to do any school work or reading and she always gets good marks, better than Dinah who is nearly at the top of the class. And she's nice to everyone even though not everyone deserves it. She speaks to the teachers like they're friends; she speaks to her father like he's her brother. And she laughs at everything all the time. Queenie was born perfect.

39. Ishmael

Ishmael sits downstairs in the garage on a big tyre watching Rachel repair The Pequod.

She slides underneath on a trolley with an enormous spanner and as she works Ahab keeps telling her what to do. He steadies himself on the wall, asking her what she can see and how the damage was caused, and without giving her any time to answer he tells her about all the restorations and repairs he did after he bought it.

'Wreck, that's what it was but the bloke that sold it to me said I could have it for eight hundred pounds. I told him it would be worth ten times that when it was repaired but he wasn't interested so I—'

'Yes, you said, Ahab,' says Rachel from underneath.

'What I'm trying to say is I didn't fool him. I told him it would be valuable and he said fair enough. The Pequod, that's what I called it, after a ship I read about in a book. It was lovely before the crash.'

'Let me guess,' shouts Rachel. 'Took the engine out, stripped it back.'

'Getting the wiring harness out was—'

'I can imagine.'

'New transmission, rock guards under the wheel trims.'

'I can see.'

'Kept the original rad fan but—'

Rachel suddenly slides out from underneath, rips her goggles off and sits up. 'Ahab, I know how to restore an engine. I was working on engines before you were. And I work on cars, vans, trucks and lorries every day. Day in. Day out. But the thing is, I only see my brother once every two bloody years. So if it's all the same to you, I'd rather talk about something else.'

'Like?'

'Like why are you here? I mean, is it a visit or is something wrong? And what's wrong with your leg? Where's the prosthetic? You've been in agony, what's going on?'

'My leg's in a white van. I'm trying to catch up with a white van. The leg's inside.'

'It's true,' says Ishmael. 'Someone came and stole it.'

Ahab closes his eyes, shakes his head. 'You should have seen it, Rachel. Big white 1973 VW Westfalia camper. Must have been a custom order originally. Completely unique. A one-off. Don't know where it came from. The only other van I ever saw like that was the one I had in ninety-nine. Remember it?'

'Course I remember. You loved that bloody van.'

'Anyway, guy named Richards from down south came up to the farmhouse with it and we struck a deal. I worked on it solidly for weeks, months maybe. Don't know why but I couldn't stop. I brought it back to life, put my heart and soul into it. Took the rust off the sides, custom-made the body panels. Gleaming it was when it was finished. I polished it until it shone. White as a ghost.'

'Why . . .?'

'Interior just needed finishing. I'd machined the wood for the extra-wide table. Waxed and polished it, white trim. The last thing. The tiny last bit. But I couldn't get to the . . . the . . .'

'Main pillar?

'The main pillar, yes, but if I took off my leg . . . it was killing me anyway. Been on it too much and it had blistered. The blisters burst, weeping, infected. The ointment doesn't help. It was just getting worse. I was working so hard I fell asleep in my clothes most nights, left it on and that's a mistake. My knee was all swollen up but I kept going. It got under my skin, right in here.' He taps his chest. 'Thought it might be my last job.'

'What do you mean, last job?'

'I don't know, just felt if I could just get it done, if I could just make it perfect then maybe I . . . I don't know. Makes no sense really. Felt like I was just coming to the end of something. I felt close to it, it felt part of me. Maybe it was the memories. Anyway, took the leg off and put it on the side. Got the table screwed on. Finished. Can't tell you how good it was.'

Ahab's voice is different. He's not shouting, he's not complaining. 'But I was tired. I had a crutch in the van already. Been using it to prop the door open. Spring catch had gone. Last little job. Fix the spring catch. Thought to myself, 'Take it off. Go inside, have a lie-down.' So I did. It was too dark to see anyway. Only meant to have a nap. Then I'd go back, get the leg, lock up. But I had a drink, just one. Knocked me out because of the painkillers. Next thing I knew it was morning.'

'Go on,' says Rachel.

'It was gone. Stolen. He came and took it. Richards. I know it was him because he had the other keys. Still got mine.'

'Bastard,' says Jude under her breath. She walks over to Ahab and puts her arms around him. He holds her with his free arm.

'It was the same van I had when I met Caroline. Felt like, if I told her. Or if she could just . . .'

He puts one hand over his eyes and Ishmael sees his body shake. She remembers how she made him go from two hundred to four hundred pounds. Remembers him telling her to hurry up and Ishmael feels bad.

'We've got the address if we can't catch him,' Ishmael says.

'It's not the money, Rachel, honest. I put my heart and soul into it.'

'And your leg,' says Ishmael and to her surprise they both burst out laughing.

'Right!' says Rachel. 'I'm coming with you.'

'No, no,' says Ahab, wiping a sleeve across his face. 'Ishmael is with me. We're fine. She's a good driver.' He points at the damage to The Pequod. 'This wasn't her fault. I'd been sleeping and not doing my bit.'

'We were going downhill,' says Ishmael.

Rachel looks from Ahab to Ishmael and claps her hands together. 'OK, right. Let's get The Pequod on the road, quick as possible. Get you all back on the road.'

She drops on to the trolley and slides back under the van. She shouts from underneath. 'You're on tea duty, Ishmael. Lots of it.'

Ishmael helps Ahab on to the tyre chair and as she climbs the stairs she hears them both talking about engines, comparing oil and tools, finishing each other's sentences, arguing about epoxy powder coatings, trims and interiors, words Ishmael has never heard before, but every so often Ahab roars with laughter and it's Rachel's turn to swear.

Jude is upstairs. When she sees Ishmael, she puts the kettle on. 'Been sent up for the tea, I expect.'

'They're talking about cars,' says Ishmael.

'Language of love for those two,' says Jude, smiling.

'Ahab was getting upset.'

'Yup.'

'He's usually just angry. I suppose upset and angry are the same thing.'

'Two sides of the same coin.'

'Like love and hate?'

'Exactly right. You know like when there's that boy at school and you say you can't stand him but really you fancy him like mad.'

Ishmael smiles. 'Or girl.'

'Or girl. Or boy. Or boy then girl. Or girl, then boy, then girl again.'

'Person,' says Ishmael.

Jude winks. 'Right again.'

Ishmael washes the cups, plates and spoons and then carefully goes back downstairs with a huge tray. Three mugs, three hunks of French bread, soft cheese, bowl of little tomatoes, packet of biscuits, chocolate bars.

'Jude says you have to have the savoury stuff first, before the sweet things. And, Ahab, you have to take the next lot of tablets. And, Rachel, you have to wash your hands.'

'Bloody hell,' says Rachel. 'She's turned into Jude's Mini Me.'

By two o'clock The Pequod is ready. Rachel opens the garage doors and helps Ahab into the passenger seat.

'You're forty miles from Jonah, Ahab,' she says. 'Forty miles between you and your boy. Think about it.'

'I want the white van, Rachel. I have to have it.'

'You know you're not making sense, Ahab. It's just a van. A pile of metal. Jonah is a living and breathing thing. Your son.'

'I have to.'

Rachel slams the door and bangs the side. 'I'll be here when you get back. Go safely.'

Jude comes round to the other side of the van and leans in. She puts a necklace over Ishmael's head. 'Take care of him, my lovely. Come this way again on your way back. I'll be here. We can talk. And remember what I said. Find your tribe.'

Ishmael looks down. The necklace is a lump of black granite on a leather strap. It feels good and heavy, smooth in her hand, but when she looks closer she sees there is a bird carved into one side, its wings outstretched and a dark yellow stone set into the granite for its eye.

Ishmael presses it to her chest. It gives her hope.

40. Dinah

Suddenly Queenie sits up, crosses her legs. The white sun streams through her bedroom window and shines through her hair. She couldn't look any more beautiful.

'You know who likes you?' she says.

Maybe this is the only thing that Dinah doesn't like about Queenie. She's always talking about boys and who likes who and who she would go out with if she had the chance.

'Who?'

'Lucas.'

'He doesn't.'

'I swear! Lucas Hammond. Don't tell me you didn't know? Everyone knows. You can tell. He's always standing with us these days and when you say anything he always jumps in. Don't you like him? He's lush.'

'No.'

'You're crazy, Dinah! You'd look amazing together. He's not like some of the idiots in Year 13. And he's eighteen. And he's got those eyes.'

'He's nice and everything but he's . . .'

'OK, OK, what is your type? Before Lucas it was Freddie and that was a no. And then Gee but OK, he's a bit of a perv. He's got the Oakfield Syndrome.'

'What's that?'

'Oh, I forgot you weren't here when Mr Oakfield got arrested. He was the games teacher in the lower school and he was always walking around in a tracksuit or a tight T-shirt and he just had this way of looking at the girls. Like he was sort of looking through your clothes.' Queenie shudders. 'He used to gross me out.'

She jumps up off the bed and goes to her wardrobe. 'Look what I bought.'

She brings out a long, colourful hippy dress. It has metres and metres of material and no sleeves, just a bodice that ties at the back.

'It's for Portugal. I'll try it on.'

She opens the door to her bathroom and disappears. 'Hmmm,' she says. 'What do you think, bra or no bra?'

Dinah gets up and looks at Queenie in the mirror. Her throat goes dry. She's wearing the dress but it's see-through. Dinah can't speak.

'If I wear a bra, the straps will show. It looks better without, doesn't it?'

Dinah nods.

'So no bra?'

'No,' whispers Dinah. 'No.'

'Can you tie it up at the back for me?'

Queenie turns round and Dinah picks up the two straps. She can see Queenie's smooth skin and she can't help but touch it.

Queenie giggles. 'Don't! I'm ticklish.'

'Sorry,' says Dinah. She ties the dress quickly and takes a deep breath.

Queenie peers into the mirror. 'I might grow my hair like yours. Not that it will look that good but I think I'll try. What do you think?'

Dinah nods and goes back to sit on the bed. Now is the time to tell Queenie how she feels. She just needs to find the right words.

Then Queenie turns round and leans round the bathroom door.

'Talking of Gee, remember when he tried to kiss you at Christmas. Oh. My. God! I thought you were going to be sick.'

Queenie gets off the bed and starts walking like Gee, talking like Gee, swaggering around the bedroom with her shoulders hunched. '*Dinah, babes, you look hot, know what I mean, babes?*'

Dinah tries to laugh but all she can see is Queenie and her body through the thin material.

'*Dinah, babes, think you and me could get it onnnnnnnn?*'

Queenie hovers over Dinah on the bed. She pouts her lips and comes close to Dinah, so close Dinah can see into her dark eyes.

'*Dinah, babes, kiss me.*'

So she does. Dinah grabs Queenie's shoulders, feels her soft skin and the silky bodice of her dress. She puts her lips against Queenie's lips and kisses her, hard, the thing she has dreamt about and wanted to do for six long months.

Queenie jumps to the other side of the room.

'What are you doing, Dinah?'

'Sorry.'

'You can't think . . .'

Dinah sat up on the bed. 'Queenie, I . . .'

'I didn't know you were a lesbian!'

'I'm not!'

'Well you just kissed me.'

'It was an accident.'

'No it wasn't. And I'm not gay, Dinah. I'm not gay, all right?'

'I know. Nor me.'

'I mean, I like boys. Boys, Dinah. Boys.'

'So do I.'

'I don't think so. I saw the way you were looking at me. And did you just touch my back? You're like him, like Oakfield.'

'I'm not! I just . . .'

'God, is that why you were looking at me?' Queenie folds her arms over her chest.

The room is spinning and Dinah is suddenly way too hot. She is trapped here in Queenie's house. Her mum isn't coming for her, because she's away on her retreat, and she's miles from anywhere. She has to get away. But Queenie's standing in front of the door.

Dinah stuffs her feet in her trainers and grabs her bag.

Queenie moves aside and Dinah runs. She runs downstairs, she runs down the drive. It was just one moment. What has she done? Ruined everything in one moment. She runs and runs until she is on the outskirts of town. It's an assault. It's against the law. She's got breath left. She has to stop. She walks as fast as she can along the dual carriageway and through the underpass that everyone knows is really dangerous but Dinah can't even see where she's going. What was she thinking? Why did she do it? One kiss. She wipes her sleeve across her face until her cheeks are sore and her eyes burn. Then she wipes her sleeve across her lips and remembers the feel of Queenie's mouth hard on hers. Oh God, oh God! It takes her two hours to walk home. Her house feels empty with her mother away.

She locks the door behind her. What if Queenie's told the police? What if Queenie tells everyone she's got Oakfield Syndrome? What if she tells her dad?

They could all be coming for her now. She runs upstairs and looks out of the window but there are no police cars. No sirens.

Maybe Queenie will wait until tomorrow. Maybe she'll just get on the phone, on the internet, and start a chat about it. It will go viral. The weird lesbian. The sexual assault. But it wasn't. It was just . . . what was it?

Five seconds is what it was and that five seconds changed everything. Queenie's face was one she'd never seen before. Horror, confusion, shock. Her mouth pulled down at the side.

She walks round and round her room. Maybe she should go back, walk two hours to Queenie's house and speak to her properly.

'I think about you all the time,' she could say. 'I wasn't thinking straight,' she could say. 'Forgive me,' she could say. 'I couldn't help it. I'm sorry.'

But there's no one in the room to hear, no one she can tell.

Dinah doesn't sleep at all that night. She lies in her bed with her eyes open, thinking about what she did, her mind and heart in agony. How can she go back to school now? What if Queenie tells everyone? She's lost Queenie. She's even lost herself.

She can never go back to school. Even if Queenie doesn't tell the police, she will tell someone who will tell someone who will tell someone else. She imagines Lily and Layla sniggering in the common room. 'Clothes Bank is a Lezzer! Clothes Bank is a Perv!'

Dinah shakes her head all the time as if to throw the images away but they don't go anywhere. She can see all the other kids and even the teachers whispering in corners, writing it on notes and passing it around. 'The strange girl is gay.' She knows if she ever goes back to school her life will be unbearable. But if she never goes back to school she will never see Queenie again and she has been the best thing in Dinah's life for years and years.

Queenie only likes boys. She made that clear. She's always talking about the boys at school and who she wants to go out with. She'll never love a girl, she'll never love Dinah. They can never be together.

Dinah has ruined everything. And there's no way to put it right. Why did she ever think she could be happy at school? Why didn't her mother insist that she stayed at home? Why didn't she listen? She was never going to fit in and now she'll be the talk of the school. The whispers. The gossip. All about her. There's no way Dinah can ever go back. There's no way she can stay around after what she's done.

She has to leave and never come back.

41. Ishmael

'What did you mean, a twenty-first birthday party?' says Ishmael.

They've been back on the road for about an hour and she remembers what he said to Sumo.

'That's where the van's going to be,' Ahab replies with the map spread out on his lap. 'Another few hours at most. We'll be there.'

'How do you know?'

'I just do. That's what he said.'

'Who?'

'Richards. The guy who stole the van. Look, never mind. That's where he's taking it. If we get there before seven then . . .'

'But why did he steal your van for a party?'

'Talking of Simon, you seemed to get on very well with his apprentice.'

The phone number! She turns her hand over but there is nothing there. The washing-up at Rachel's house. She's washed the number away and now it's gone for ever. She'll never see him again.

'What was his name?' says Ahab.

'Pip.'

'What's up?'

'Nothing.'

'What is it?'

'I don't want to talk about it,' Ishmael says, and they drive in silence after that.

It's hours along the Fosse Way. The road is dead straight and Ishmael can see ahead for miles and miles. Tall trees arch their branches, holding hands over the road lined with bushes and brambles. Tall blue flowers whip the windows of The Pequod if she gets too close to the edge. The sun is just dipping down behind the golden fields; the sky is shot through with pink and purple, silver clouds streaking across it like something from Gabriel's painting. She remembers the raven's wing and her message. Rebirth. She touches the granite necklace from Jude. Find your tribe.

She looks up at the mirror in front of her and pulls her hat off. Bald. She rubs her hand across her scalp and remembers the feel of Pip's hand on her new skin, on her neck, and the way he walked, slow and easy. Again, the flutter in her belly. She'll never see him again.

Then they both see it together, the sign for Avoncliff. The sign for the village where Jonah lives with Tego and Caroline. Where the new baby lives.

'Ishmael, take the next on the right.'

'Avoncliff is on the left, Ahab. We could—'

'Go right. We're nearly there.'

Ishmael turns right. They're in a village with a row of shops and a train station. They pass a church and a graveyard and then it's open country again, driving away from Avoncliff.

'Look!' Ahab points to a huge white marquee in a field. It's the biggest tent Ishmael's ever seen, with three peaks in the roof and great big windows and hundreds of little flags on top. There are dozens of people milling around outside and as they get nearer they can hear music and laughter.

'That's it! It must be.'

Ishmael looks in her rear-view mirror to check the traffic behind her and she sees a long line of vehicles. She adjusts the mirror again because it's hard to believe.

'Ahab,' she says. 'Look behind.'

He turns in his seat. 'My God.'

Ishmael slows down and pulls over to the side of the road to let them pass.

Campervans. Ten, fifteen, maybe twenty. Every colour, blue, orange, green, red, purple. Ahab announces each one as they pass.

'1975, I think T2. 1976 Westfalia, left-hand drive, California probably. 2 litre Berlin, nice. 1970 Viking Roof. Rare.'

They all pass but he is not there, Richards and the white van are not with them.

The campervans snake off down the road, a beautiful multi-coloured string of them turning into the field with the marquee.

'Quick!' says Ahab. 'Join on the end.'

The Pequod pulls into the road after them. She drives down a dirt track and joins the convoy of campervans that circle the marquee sounding their horns in a deafening symphony. Ishmael bangs on the horn of The Pequod.

'What are you doing?' says Ahab.

'Just fitting in.'

People flood out of the tent, clapping and waving. There's music playing from enormous speakers and tables and chairs everywhere and fairy lights in blue and yellow hanging from the branches of tall trees. And in the centre of the crowd there's a young woman in a flowing summer dress that matches her hair, long and white. She wears a headdress of white flowers like some medieval princess and the sun seems to sparkle around her, shines on her bare arms and shoulders. She's beautiful. When she sees the crescent of campervans, she brings her hands up to her face and gasps. She looks overwhelmed with happiness.

Then one by one the campervans slow down and start parking in a crescent, perfectly choreographed around the entrance to the tent. Ishmael copies the van ahead and parks carefully at the end.

The drivers are getting out, smiling and waving, all of them dressed for a party with presents and bunches of flowers, and now Ishmael notices that even the campervans themselves have ribbons tied around them like they're going to a wedding. The Pequod, with its damaged front and dirty wheels, stands out a mile. Ahab looks like a tramp and Ishmael is wearing joggers and a hoodie. If they get out everyone will notice.

Then, through the entrance to the field, a beautiful whale white campervan drives into the field all on its own. It's tied around with rainbow streamers and bows and a big balloon on the top that's waving in the wind. '21' it says and Ishmael knows it's Ahab's van.

The girl is jumping up and down as it makes its way slowly over the grass and comes to a stop right in front of her. The whole crowd surges forward and begins to clap.

'It's your van, Ahab!' Ishmael whispers. 'Isn't it?'

'It is,' he answers. 'That's Richards, all right.'

The white van stops right in front of the beautiful girl and the driver gets out.

He's a big man, Richards, the thief. He's got short red hair and a big curly beard. He's wearing a grey and white check shirt that billows like a sail in the wind.

226

'Happy Birthday, my love,' he says. He gives her a long hug and everyone cheers. 'Hoorah!'

Richards holds his hands up and everyone goes quiet.

'Thank you everyone for coming this evening. Thanks to the Avoncliff Van Club, thanks to the caterers and everyone that's come along for Emily's twenty-first birthday party.'

There are cheers again and Richards has to shout to be heard. Ishmael watches Ahab, the set of his jaw, his chest going up and down with the fury she has seen before.

Richards continues. 'As some of you already know, she hasn't had an easy time lately, my Emily. She's not been well and she's needed a bit of looking after.'

There are murmurs in the crowd and Emily goes and stands by her father.

'But look at her now, eh? As beautiful as the day she was born, if that's possible.'

'Hear, hear,' says someone.

'You'll all know she's loved these vans since she was a little girl. Always been her intention to have one, so, I found one. This beauty here. And today, Emily love, on your twenty-first birthday, I present you with your very own VW campervan.'

There are shouts and cheers and suddenly everyone bursts into song.

'Happy Birthday to you! Happy Birthday to you! Happy Birthday, dear Emily. Happy Birthday to you!'

Slowly, Ishmael opens her door and slips out of The Pequod. Ahab does the same, holding on carefully to the wing mirror. Ishmael helps him shuffle through the crowd until they are nearly at the front. As they pass, people look them up and down. They don't belong and everyone knows it.

But Emily is smiling and looking from one face to another, saying, 'Thank you, thank you,' and then her father holds the key in the air and just before he gives it to her he holds his hands up for quiet again.

'As you'll know better than me, all campervans have names. So, Emily, what will you call it?'

Emily looks past her father and off down the track that leads to the field and her whole face lights up.

'Jonah,' she says, under her breath, and then louder. 'I'll call it Jonah! Jonah!'

It's impossible but it's true. Walking towards the crowd is Jonah. The same Jonah but taller and dressed in a black suit like he's going to a wedding. Ishmael's heart turns over and she feels Ahab's whole body go rigid.

'My God,' he whispers. 'I knew it. I knew he'd be here.'

Jonah starts to jog when he sees everybody looking and Emily runs towards him and when they meet he picks her up and spins her around. Then he puts her down and kisses her. Cheering. More cheering.

'Oh, what a lovely couple,' says a woman next to her.

'Don't they suit each other?' says another.

Ishmael can only watch as they walk hand in hand back to the middle of the crowd. Jonah in love, a stupid romantic scene like something from a film. Richards puts his arm around Jonah's shoulder and gives him a big hug.

'Everyone knows this young man, Jonah! It was his idea in the first place, he found the van and even found somewhere to have it mended. Take a bow, my boy!'

Jonah is smiling and when the clapping dies down, someone says, 'Speech! Speech!'

Jonah's a bit embarrassed but he coughs and starts.

'Just want to say thanks to Emily's dad for everything. For giving me a job at the farm, which I start in a few weeks, thanks for that, and for making me welcome into the family, and for welcoming my mum and dad too . . .'

Ishmael feels Ahab lurch forward. This is too much for him and she can't hold him back. He elbows his way to the front of the crowd and bellows as loud as he can.

'Richards, you bastard!'

There's silence and Ishmael closes her eyes. She doesn't want to see Jonah's face. She doesn't want to see everyone looking at them in the wrong clothes, with her bald head and Ahab all scruffy.

'Dad?' Jonah sounds suddenly like a little boy. 'Dinah, is that you?' Ishmael opens her eyes and he is there in front of her looking completely confused.

'What's going on here?' says Richards and then he seems to recognise Ahab. 'You!' he shouts. 'What the hell are you doing here?'

Ishmael can hear people muttering to one another. 'He's got one leg?' 'Who are they?' 'Who brought that old van in here?'

But Ahab has only just started. He grabs Ishmael's shoulder with one hand to steady himself and with the other he points at Richards, jabbing the air between them.

'You owe me money!' he shouts.

Richards towers over them. He moves Emily to one side and faces Ahab square on. Ishmael sees the anger in his eyes.

'Me? You talking to me?'

'Yes you,' says Ahab, looking up at him. 'No money. No van. That van is mine.'

'You've lost it, mate,' Richards says, shaking his head. 'That van belongs to me.'

Ishmael is right between them and any minute now they're going to start fighting but Jonah separates them, one hand on the chest of each man.

'Stop it!'

Emily is at his side, pulling at her father's sleeve. 'Dad, Dad!'

And all the time the crowd are looking at them, wondering who they are, the people that have come and ruined Emily's party, the people nobody knows. They should know the truth.

230

'You stole his van!' Ishmael says to Richards. 'We're going to call the police.'

'Ha!' says Richards and pretends to laugh. He turns to the crowd and holds his hands wide open. 'Have you heard this?'

He faces Ahab and shakes his head. 'I gave you that van to fix, mate. Not to buy. And you damn well know it. It was this one here that recommended you. If I'd known you were barmy I'd never have given you the job.'

Jonah hangs his head. He looks ashamed. 'I'm sorry,' he says to Richards. 'I should have told you he's my father.'

People start to murmur as though they can't believe it. Jonah is red with embarrassment.

'Him? This deadbeat?' Richards says.

'I thought for a minute he'd somehow come to see me, but you haven't, have you, Dad?'

Ahab turns his face away. 'I've come for what's mine. He stole that van and I want it back.'

'I stole nothing,' says Richards. 'I told him that I needed it back in six weeks and every time I rang up it was the same story. "It's not finished. It's not finished." A bit more time, he said. Something about the original door handle, the exact match on the curtains and the trim, the wheel arch being chrome and not plastic. I said he was a right pain in the arse, and now he's come here and ruined Emily's bloody party!'

He makes a quick movement towards Ahab and Ahab loses his balance and ends up on the floor. He rolls around but can't get up. Jonah tries to help but Ahab shrugs him off.

'Leave me alone! Everyone leave me alone!'

People start to whisper to one another. 'Is he drunk?' 'Who invited him?' 'He's a troublemaker.' 'Should we call the police?' The whole party is in a circle looking at Ahab on the ground. He looks ridiculous, angry and dirty, swearing and trying to get up all on his own.

Ishmael looks at Jonah and sees the shame written on his face. 'I'm sorry,' she says.

'It's not your fault,' he answers but he's staring at her. 'What's happened? I mean, your hair and everything? You look . . .'

Emily is watching them. She looks at Jonah and says, 'How do you two know each other?'

'She's just my other sister,' he says, and Ishmael feels the words slap her in the face.

Just his other sister? Just his other sister!

And then, just when she thought it couldn't all get any worse, Ishmael sees her father, and Caroline, and their new baby, coming across the field towards them. Ishmael simply can't face them, especially not now.

She steps back, nearly tripping over Ahab, who looks pathetic, all covered in mud and unable to stand.

He looks up at her and holds out his hand. 'Help me up then.'

And in that moment, she hates him, hates him for putting her in this situation, for making fools of them both, for lying about his van being stolen.

She turns away from him and runs. Her leg is still hurting but not as much as her heart, so she runs.

'Hey!' he shouts. 'Come back!'

'Dinah!' shouts Jonah.

She runs, ignoring him, runs past The Pequod and across the field.

Ishmael sprints into the lane. She turns around but no one's behind her. She keeps running, faster still, and feels her lungs straining for air. She almost trips. Faster. 'My other sister.' Is that all she is now? Not the only sister. Not even that.

She runs until she runs out of breath. She's so hot she could faint. She pulls her jumper off and stops by the graveyard. She walks through the gate and down a narrow path where the trees shade a wooden bench. She almost falls on to it she is so tired. She leans back and tries to calm down.

She's run away from everyone now. From school, from Queenie. From her father and Caroline and their new baby, from Jonah and his new girlfriend, from Ahab and from her mother. There is no one else to run from and nowhere to run to. It's the end of the road.

And what was it all for? She thought she was running away from Queenie, from a kiss, from a mistake. But she's brought it all with her. She could have stayed and said sorry. She could have explained. All this way for nothing. She thought she was running away from her father, from Caroline, from Jonah, but she's run straight into them again.

She puts both hands over head and feels her bald, damp, sweating scalp. Her hair. Her beautiful hair, gone. And for what? She could run and run and run and she would never run away from who she really is.

She remembers the last time she went to see her father. Caroline was pregnant. She wafted around in a long green dress, her hair in a long plait down her back.

Their new house was just like New Bedford recreated. Pots and pots of flowers, tubs of herbs and leaves for cooking and eating, for medicine and drying, bits of tree and bark for marvelling at, for wondering about nature, for teaching children about how things grow and how they should be protected in the world. And Caroline pregnant and lovely and her father with his hand on her belly, singing to the new life inside.

A cosy cottage for everyone except her, lots of places to sit and lie, for talking and being silent, and pure chaos everywhere else, dishes that aren't washed, clothes in baskets, piles of magazines and books, a guitar, another guitar, windows wide open, a loaf of bread half cut on a breadboard on the table, a tapestry hanging lopsided on the wall and the smell of yeast and sap and lives full of energy and love.

And now there is a new child living there. A new special girl for her father. A new sister for Jonah, and Ishmael belongs nowhere.

She can hardly see in this quiet corner of the graveyard. It's nearly dark and the sky has turned an angry purple, no stars, no moon.

And then next she hears the sound of a raven's caw. She looks up. It sits on a branch looking at her. Then it flutters down beside her. Ishmael holds her breath. She mustn't frighten it away.

The raven is as still and quiet as the granite one that lies on Ishmael's chest. It sits and sits and then suddenly it turns and looks at her with its deep yellow eyes. 'I know,' it seems to say. 'I know.'

And then Ishmael starts to cry. All the tears she has saved up since she kissed Queenie, since Ahab shouted at her, since she crashed the van and cut her head shaving, since she vowed never to cry again and promised that she would make herself into someone else. Tears when she thinks of her hair coiled in the bottom of her bag, all for nothing, all over one kiss. She cries all the tears she didn't cry when her father left and some of the ones that she did. The tears of shame from wearing the wrong clothes at school and the cruel things that the other kids said. The hot tears she would have cried if Queenie would have loved her back and the hot tears of regret now she knows she never will. All the tears she would have cried if Jonah had hugged her instead of the beautiful Emily with the long hair and the crown of flowers. All the happy tears she could have shed at having a baby sister if she really, honestly and truly believed that she still mattered to her father, if she still had a place in his world. And she cries for the way Pip made her feel. Find your tribe, said Jude, but Ishmael has no tribe, she's in between, always on the outside, neither one thing nor the other, nothing good ever happens and nobody wants her.

Ishmael cries into her hands and cannot stop. Her chest is heaving and her throat is straining from the noise she makes.

And then she thinks of her mother and her brave face and her kindness. And Ishmael cries because she refused to go to the Sacred Women Retreat and her mother is all alone and doesn't know that she is loved and missed because Ishmael never tells her any more. She cries because her mother was the only one who looked after Ahab and nursed him back to health, who helped him walk again and washed his clothes.

And she cries for Ahab's leg and the pain it causes him and the way he tries to be strong. She cries for him being stuck back there, in the mud, humiliated. She cries because she left him. She cries because he probably really believed the van belonged to him, really believed it would win Caroline back. And now he knows that Caroline has a new baby and she will never be his again. And the more Ishmael cries the more she thinks she will never stop. She is crying from the bottom of her soul and there are more tears there than all the water in the Golden Lake.

But, eventually, Ishmael remembers the raven. She drags her sleeve across her eyes. It must have flown away with all the noise Ishmael's been making but no, it's there. Sitting still, watching.

The raven cocks its head to one side. It looks like a question. 'Well? What now?'

Ishmael shakes her head. 'I don't know what to do.'

The raven flies to the gate of the graveyard and sits on the wall. Ishmael picks up her jumper and follows. She walks down the path, past all the people who have died and been buried, all the people who have no more life to live, and as she walks past she thinks how much they would give to have one more day, to have the life that's inside her right now. What would they do with it?

When she gets to the gate, the raven flies to the edge of the village and Ishmael follows. She walks past the little shops all clustered together and gets to the railway station.

The raven sits on the white metal railings and looks right and looks left. To the left is a fast train waiting by the platform. A train that will take her to freedom, a new life, with her new name, not having to rely on anyone, not having to answer to anyone, ever. A life alone, starting again and running away. And to the right is Ahab, and Jonah, and his new girlfriend, and Tego and Caroline, and their new baby, and, beyond that, her mother, surely angry about Ishmael running away, and Queenie, who must hate her. Is it really worth the hurt, the pain, of going back and having to face them all again?

Ishmael runs her fingers across her stubbly head, the hair already beginning to grow back, and watches the raven spread its velvet wings like it's waving goodbye as it soars high above the village, black against the darkening sky. Ishmael watches until it's gone. Now she knows now what she must do, where she needs to be.

She places her hand over her heart and bows to the raven.

'Thank you,' she says.

Epilogue

You walk into school and you know everyone's looking but you keep your eyes straight ahead. It took you weeks to find the courage to go back. You thought you would never have the nerve but in the end they talked you into it. Jude made the three-hour journey north and sat with Ahab and your mother at the kitchen table. You told them all everything. Every single thing you had done wrong and all the things you felt in your soul.

Ahab listened without saying a word good or bad.

Your mother cried a bit. 'I'm so sorry,' she said. 'I wish I'd known, Dinah,' and you don't correct her because actually Dinah is a nice name and she's the one that gave it to you and it suits you better than Ishmael after all.

Jude was the one that asked the difficult questions. 'So you're giving up, then? Not going to take your exams that you've worked so hard for? Just going to hide in your bedroom?'

You've got no answers, only shame.

'You made a stupid mistake. Are you going to make it again?'

'No.'

'And the driving without a bloody licence, Dinah,' said Jude, pointing a finger, 'what about that? And don't say anything about Ahab making you do it because I know he did and he's had a bloody good telling-off as well.'

And Ahab says he's sorry and says it's his fault.

But Jude tells him to be quiet and carries on. 'So are you doing to be breaking the law again, Dinah?'

'No.'

'That was dangerous as well as stupid.'

'Yes, I know.'

'Right, so where are you now?' said Jude. 'In there,' she poked you in the chest, 'and in there,' she poked you in the temple. 'What's your next move? What does your raven say?'

The answer comes to you in the night when you can't sleep. You write Queenie a letter and you tell her everything, how obsession got the better of you and you're sorry. You touch the granite raven on your necklace. 'Wish me luck,' you say.

You get dressed the next day and you put your school books in your bag. You take a deep breath. You take another deep breath and you take a step and then another one and there you are in front of Queenie and Queenie's face is the one you love, her eyes wide open, her lips apart. There's a moment, and the moment seems to last for ever and you don't know if she's going to smile or sneer so you have to stand there and wait while everyone looks. The best thing to do is say sorry. Again. So you start to speak. You take the letter out of your bag and hand it to her.

'I just wanted to say—'

'Wait,' she says. She takes the letter and she reads it slowly. There's just the two of you but you can't say anything. She looks up when she's finished and smiles.

She touches your scalp, except it's not skin any more, there's little prickles of hair, soft and downy, and the cuts have healed and against all the odds it looks brilliant, and it helps that you had your ears pierced because your mum bought you great big hoops that make you look 'kick-ass' and that's a new word you got from Jonah because you're friends again.

'No way!' she says. She doesn't talk about the letter or what you did wrong, she just makes you turn round and round, saying 'Wow!' all the time. And because she's not angry and because she's forgiven you and because she's still Queenie and just the best friend you could ever have, you feel like you might cry. And you wonder why it is that since you cut your hair you've cried about three times but you never did before? And if there's an answer you don't really care because Queenie gives you the biggest hug and whispers in your ear, 'Missed you.'

And all through break and dinnertime you tell her about the gig you went to and Pip with the Afro and the way Ahab had Sumo's phone number all along and took you there in the van, and when Pip saw you he put his arms around you like you'd been friends for ever. More than friends. And Queenie looks at you a bit funny and

241

says she didn't know you liked boys as well and you smile and say, 'Me neither,' and then you both start laughing and no one else gets the joke so that makes it worse and you both laugh until your eyes water. And that's another way to cry but a good one.

You did turn back. You did turn right. You did what you thought you'd never have the strength to do but somehow you found it.

You walked all the way back to the field the way the raven flew and they were all there waiting, all there worried about you. You went straight to the baby in Caroline's arms and you stared and stared. You realise your sister has done nothing wrong, she's sweet and innocent and looks like all your baby photos, and no matter how she came into the world, she will always be part of you. So you forgive her for being born and you forgive Jonah for loving her too.

And your father puts his arms around you and holds you and, for the first time since he left, you hold him back. And you ask for time to deal with the rest, with Caroline and your father's new life. And Ahab shakes your father's hand and somehow things start slotting into place like the very end of a jigsaw when little pieces can only go in one place and it all looks obvious and easy.

And then Ahab straps on his leg and drives you north in The Pequod in a quieter voice that's almost kind.

You come back to life. Becoming Dinah again.

And then Ahab comes down the track and asks if you want a job. 'Engineer,' he says, 'or mechanic, call it what you like. Start Saturday. Eight sharp. Don't be late.'

But he stands at the front door for ages talking to your mum and saying good things about you that he never said to your face. And he stays so long that he ends up eating dinner with you and your mum and trying to make conversation like a normal person.

And tonight you'll look out of your bedroom window and you'll look for a raven. Maybe you will see one, maybe you won't. But over the fields towards the factory and the motorway you'll see the winking lights and you'll hear the lorries in the distance and you'll realise that the road that took you away has led you all the way back home.

Author's Note

Moby Dick is a story about obsession and finding yourself. The original book was told by Ishmael, a sailor who embarks on Captain Ahab's quest to find the white whale that bit off his leg. It's a gripping and exciting story that takes place mostly on The Pequod, Ahab's ship on dangerous foreign seas. What is remarkable about this book is that it features so many different nationalities, (the sailors came from all over the world) and religions and respect for other faiths as well as a close relationship between Ishmael and another sailor, Quepeg. But there are no women in Moby Dick; some wives wave The Pequod out of port but that's basically it. I wanted to change all that. I wanted to make Ishmael female and have it all told from her point of view. I wanted her to try and succeed in wrestling control away from Ahab on the journey, to become fully herself, free of religion, free of her mistakes, free of her past, and in Becoming Dinah she begins to realise who she is and to be proud of that. Dinah/Ishmael is *Moby Dick* for now and for all the girls and women who are on a journey to self-discovery.

Kit de Waal

Acknowledgements

My first thanks go to Herman Melville for writing *Moby Dick*, a book I have read and loved and read again. He inspired me to think about obsession and grief and helped me know Dinah and her journey back to herself.

I would also like to thank Jackie Hagan who helped me understand Ahab's disability, what he could and couldn't do and how that would make him feel. Ely Percy, a great writer and friend, talked to me and sent me extensive notes about Dinah's sexuality and sexual identity and how that impacts young people. Their help is very much appreciated.

Adam Sharp, novelist and friend, was patient and kind and kept me company and in constant gin supply in Cromarty where much of this novel was written. Thank you also to Cromarty Arts Trust.

To everyone that I bored with details of vintage

campervans and the minutiae of restoration: thank you and it's over now. As you were.

To Jo Unwin, thank you always for your advice on things literary, professional and personal. And to Helen Thomas, editor extraordinaire, my deepest gratitude for your wise and incisive suggestions and your help and guidance in making this novel the best it could be. I'm very lucky to have you with me.

As always to my sisters Kim, Tracey and Karen and brothers Conrad and Dean, love to you always.

This and everything else I do will always be for my children, Bethany and Luke. Love you Crumplefoot. Love you Badgie.

And to Leah Doyle, hope you like it!

BELLATRIX *[noun: female warrior]*

In literature and in life, women of the past and present
have a million stories that are untold, mis-told or unheard.
In response, we are proud to launch Bellatrix:
a new collection of gripping, powerful and diverse YA
novels by leading female voices. From gothic to thriller
to romance to funny, each book is entirely unique,
but linked by a passion for telling *her whole story*.

HER STORY
THE WHOLE STORY